THE EARL

OF

DEVERON

Sons of the Marquess

Book 0

A Regency Story

by Mary Kingswood

Sons of the Marquess Book 0: The Earl of Deveron

Published by Sutors Publishing

ISBN: 978-1-912167-24-1 (paperback)

V2

Cover design by: Shayne Rutherford of Darkmoon Graphics

Sons of the Marquess Book 0: The Earl of Deveron

About this book: *A traditional Regency romance, drawing room rather than bedroom.*

The Earl of Deveron is shocked when his father dies unexpectedly. Left alone to struggle with his new responsibilities, he is delighted when a childhood friend returns to his life to banish his loneliness. But Beatrice Mallory's intentions are not entirely altruistic, and when she sets out to ensnare her old friend into marriage, he will need to dream up a very clever scheme to escape her wiles.

About the series Sons of the Marquess: *the ninth Marquess of Carrbridge is happily married to the former Miss Constance Allamont, he has an heir and a spare in the nursery, and all seems set fair for a life of perfect bliss. His five younger brothers are a bit of a handful, but young men like to spread their wings a bit. If only they weren't so expensive! And whatever happened to that huge income his father used to boast about? It seems to have vanished in a generation. And now there's the unknown son of his father's who claims to be the legitimate heir. It's all a bit much for an easy-going marquess to deal with. Fortunately, his wife has some ideas about restoring their fortunes...*

Book 0: The Earl of Deveron (a prequel novella, free to mailing list subscribers)

Book 1: Lord Reginald

Book 2: Lord Humphrey

Book 3: Lord Augustus

Book 4: Lord Montague

Book 5: Lord Gilbert

Want to be the first to hear about new releases? Sign up for my mailing list at http://marykingswood.co.uk

Sons of the Marquess Book 0: The Earl of Deveron

Table of Contents

Prologue

The ninth Marquess of Carrbridge gently lifted his wife down from the saddle.

"You are coming along splendidly," he said, smiling down at her, as grooms led away their horses, their hooves echoing in the cavernous stables of Drummoor. "No one would guess you had never sat a horse before our marriage."

He watched as she shook out the skirts of her riding habit, smoothing away an imaginary crease, blushing shyly. How pretty she looked today! She always looked pretty in his eyes, but the colour of her coat set off her complexion perfectly, and never had he seen a more fetching hat. Her taste was exquisite, and even after a canter through mud and brambles, she looked immaculate.

"Ah, Connie! How wonderful this is!" he said, sweeping her back into his arms and kissing her soundly, for he was not at all ready to release her just yet.

"The grooms, Lord Carrbridge!" she protested, as soon as she was able to speak. But laughter burst from her, and he concluded that she was not at all cross with him. "Come, let us change out of these damp clothes as soon as we may, for you must be ready for breakfast."

"Damp?" he said in alarm. "I would not have you damp for the world. Perhaps we should not have ridden so far."

"Nonsense! It was a little misty when we set off, as a November morning is likely to be."

"But you might take a chill, my sweet, and how should I ever forgive myself?"

"You worry too much, my dear. Come, let us go into the house where it is a little warmer."

"Are you cold?" he cried. "Damp and cold — it is the worst of all afflictions! Let us go inside at once, before any lasting damage may occur."

They made their way through the stables and across the chapel court to the side door that allowed them easy access to their apartments. Drummoor was a wilderness of a house, built in a time when a country estate needed to provide for every requirement, its courtyards edged with bakery and brewery, smithy and joinery and much more besides. It rambled, that was the trouble, and the marquess would not have been unhappy to quit it entirely. But Lady Carrbridge was fond of the place, liking to fill it with her friends, and her ingenuity had created a cosy little nest for them in a corner of one wing. Their bedrooms were there, and a tiny dining room so that they could enjoy a meal alone if they wished, as well as a sitting room with her paintings and tapestries on the wall, and an informal portrait of the two of them hanging above the fire.

Today they breakfasted in the winter morning room, for there were guests in the house, as was so often the case. Connie was her usual charming self, having thankfully taken no ill from the damp morning air. His greatest fear was for her health, and he watched her covertly every day for signs of any lack of appetite or want of spirits. He had never seen such signs yet, even when she had been increasing, but he could not quite restrain himself from fretting over her.

After breakfast he had the tedium of a meeting with his agent, and explaining the unexpected need for additional sums of money. Sharp was a good fellow, however, and reassured him at once that there was not the least difficulty in clearing Gil's gaming debts again, and increasing Gus's allowance. Those were always his exact words, *'...not the least difficulty, my lord'.* Then the usual profusion of bows. Sharp would never sit in his presence, the more readily to enable him to bow after every third word. And he bent so low it was a wonder his nose did not bump his knees.

Still, such excessive deference was but a small price to pay for hearing those most delightful of all words — *'...not the least difficulty.'* It was pleasant to know that the estate was so well managed, even if he could never quite understand why it was that Sharp was able to find funds at a moment's notice, when he himself never seemed to have enough in hand. Other men, he knew, could go directly to the bank for their needs, but whenever he had tried that, the manager had dolefully explained that there were but a few hundred pounds to his name. It was a mystery, but he had never had much of a head for money and as long as there was enough of it, he put it out of his thoughts.

He was so well cheered by his quick release from Sharp's obsequiousness that he decided to celebrate by visiting his wife in her sitting room. She liked to spend an hour or two each morning writing to this or that relative — she was always writing letters! She preferred to be alone, but he could write to Gil and Gus, and how charming it would be to sit side by side at their matching escritoires penning their missives. His dear Connie could not possibly object to such an enterprise.

Nor did she, turning to him with a smile as he entered the room. "Have you finished already with Mr Sharp? Ah, I can see by your countenance that it was satisfactory."

"Indeed it was, most satisfactory. I do not like begging for funds so soon after the last time, but I believe I brushed through it tolerably well, and Sharp has kindly agreed to find the necessary."

"It is your own money, my love," she said. "You need not scruple to ask for whatever you need, and Mr Sharp is obliged to provide it. He cannot refuse you the use of your own fortune."

He was very much struck by this aspect of the matter, for he had never quite considered it in such a light before. "Do you know, my sweet, that is very true. It *is* my fortune, is it not? I just wish I knew exactly how much there was of it and where it is all hidden and why I have to ask Sharp whenever I want some of it. But it is mine, and I may do with it as I please. Or as *you* please. What should you like?"

She laughed. "You know what I should like — a little phaeton of my own, so that I may drive myself around town in the most delightful manner."

"Oh, but think how dreadful it would be if you should be overturned! No, no, my sweet, it is not to be thought of. I am happy to drive you wherever you wish to go, you know, or you may take the carriage, as befits a marchioness."

"There! I knew there was not the least use in asking. But there is nothing else I wish for just now. You have showered me with jewels, I have a splendid allowance for my clothes, and the improvements to Marford House are all in hand. Once that is completed to my satisfaction, I shall turn my attention to Drummoor and then I shall ask for more money, but until then I am perfectly content."

"Are you indeed content, my little love?"

"Most certainly I am. How could it be otherwise, when I am married to the finest man in the world?"

He sighed with pleasure. "And you are the best of wives. Happy for me was the day that I met you at the Amblesides' ball, do you remember it? You talked about dragons and highwaymen and all sorts of nonsense, and I was quite enchanted. I knew at once that I wanted to marry you."

"And yet you pretended you did not," she said gently. "You led me to believe you were quite indifferent to me, that you loved another, and I was very unhappy for a while."

"It was foolish of me, I know," he said, kneeling at her feet and taking her hands in his. "My dearest Connie, I never meant to hurt you, not in the least, but I needed to be sure that you were the right wife for me. I was nearly caught once by a designing woman who only wanted my title and cared nothing for me. It frightened me so much that I swore I would never allow that to happen again. So I came up with my clever scheme of pretending to be in love with someone else, and made us both unhappy. I am not very good at clever schemes, am I? It is much better now that I can leave that sort of thing to you."

She smiled and raised one of his hands to her lips. "Poor Francis! Your scrape with this designing woman must have been very bad if you felt the need to resort to such subterfuge."

"It was!" He shuddered. "You cannot imagine..."

"Yet you never talk about it."

"Do you want to hear the story? I could not speak of it for a long time, because... I did not behave just as I ought, I feel. It would please me greatly to hear your opinion."

"Then let me send for some tea, and you may tell me all about it."

She rang the bell and gave her orders, then led him to the window seat, just wide enough for two people who liked very much to sit close to each other.

Taking her hand, he said, "I was but one and twenty, still the Earl of Deveron then, and newly down from Oxford. My brothers were all away at university or at school, and Mama was in Harrogate, taking the waters, for her health was so delicate by then. It was November, and the weather foul, when Father was struck by a sudden illness..."

1: An Untimely Death

The Earl of Deveron crept down the dark corridor, following the lamp flickering in the butler's hand. The house was so different at night, the shabby familiarity of passageways and stairs eaten up by deep shadows that loomed alarmingly. Statues sprang to monstrous life as the lamplight leapt at them, only to shrink back into their normal, nonthreatening selves as the light grew. Mysterious creaks and clicks made his heart leap about, but when he looked over his shoulder there was only darkness.

More stairs, and then the blue carpet that meant they were approaching his father's room. Crabbe stopped, tapping on the door. It opened to reveal Mr Penicuik's white face. The chaplain. Things must be very bad, then, for the marquess to send for his chaplain.

The bed dominated the room, its great canopy lost in the gloom. The curtains were drawn back to reveal a small, frail figure lying amidst the white pillows. The doctor was there, and in the shadows he saw his sister Harriet's anxious face, and her governess, quite composed. On the other side of the bed, a couple of the aunts, weeping, and in a dark corner Elkham, his father's valet, also weeping. Near the fire, Mr Sharp the agent sat in a leather wing chair, a glass of brandy in his hand.

"Come closer, my lord," Mr Penicuik said, in his soft voice, more like a girl's than a man's. "His lordship wishes to speak to you."

He ushered Dev towards the bed. There was his father, his face grey in the dim light. At least, it must be his father, for the shape of the face, the lips, the nose were all those of the eighth marquess. The nightcap was the same, even the hands reaching for him were as familiar to him as his own. But these hands shook with effort, and the eyes — no, these pain-filled orbs were not his father's.

Nor was the reedy voice. "Francis... Come here, my boy. Something... must say."

"I am here, Father."

"Closer," he whispered. Dev leaned forward a little. "Hand..." The shaking hands were hovering uncertainly in the air. Dev looked at Mr Penicuik in bewilderment.

"Take his hand, my lord," Penicuik hissed.

Dev took one hand in his. Such large hands his father had, such capable hands, whether driving his own team or shooting or playing cards with confident movements. Capable with women, too, it was said. Dev could not reconcile this sick, old man with his tall, strong father, so healthy only three days earlier. He had driven down from town in his own curricle, heedless of the November chill, laughing off the rain, striding through the house with his voice echoing, as always. That evening he had retired early, a little fatigued, he said. He had not left his bed since. And now...

"Francis..." The capable hands felt as fragile as paper. "Glad you are here, my boy... I want—" He broke off, gasping for breath, mouth wide open, the lips blue. The doctor rushed forward with a moist cloth and a glass of water, but neither were needed. The fit passed off as suddenly as it had come. "All this... soon be yours," his father whispered. "Title... estate... everything."

"Father, I am sure—"

"No. Say nothing. Must listen. Not much time. I... shall not... see the dawn, so..." He tried to catch his breath again, his breath rasping, then lay back on the pillow, eyes closed. For a moment, Dev's stomach twisted in fear, but then the eyes opened again and the voice, when it came, was a little stronger. "Francis... much sooner than we expected, but you will be all right. Good boy, always have been. But... must promise me... look after your brothers, you understand?"

"Of course, Father."

"Your sister... no need to worry about her, but your brothers... You must promise me, Francis — take care of *all* my sons. All important to me... sons of a marquess... ought to be somebody. Take care of them, all of them. Make sure they can live well — careers, that sort of thing. Never got round to it myself. Thought I had time. Promise me."

"I promise, Father."

"Good boy. Always a good boy." The eyes closed again.

"There," Mr Penicuik said. "He will be easier now that he has spoken to you, my lord, and unburdened himself. Perhaps he will sleep a little."

Dev released the hand, now limp and heavy, laying it carefully down on the bed. "Should I go now? Or stay?"

"It is as you wish, my lord. There is a chair by the fire, should you wish to stay. Or if you prefer to go to your room, you will be called at once if there is any change."

His sister Harriet appeared at his side. Harriet was nineteen, two years younger than Dev, but sometimes she seemed very wise and worldly, just like their mama.

"What should I do, Hatty?"

"Let us go to Mama's sitting room. There is a fire there, for Julia and I have been using it since Father was taken ill. Come now, Crabbe will fetch you some brandy. We can do nothing here, you know. Father is settled now that he has spoken to you, so we had best leave."

Dev allowed himself to be led away, the governess trailing behind. Their mother's sitting room was a pleasant place, a jumble of mismatched furniture that she would never replace because, she always said, every item brought back happy memories. A small stool employed to rest her feet was one that Dev himself had sat on as a child while she read stories to him from a book. The chaise longue was where she had liked to sit, the wooden cot at her side, with each successive baby. Here in a little cabinet were arrayed the miniatures of each child, the likenesses taken anew every spring. In a corner sat the box with the wooden soldiers and china dolls they had played with. Her presence lingered in the room, even though she had not been there for months. He could almost smell her perfume in the air.

"She has been told?" Dev said anxiously.

"I wrote myself as soon as the severity of Father's affliction became apparent," Harriet said. "Mama can hardly have received my letter yet, however, and she may not be able to travel for some time."

"The roads are so bad at this time of year," Dev said vaguely.

"That, and her health may not permit it. It do not think the waters have done her any good at all."

"She said she felt better," he protested. "In her last letter, I am certain she said there was some improvement."

"You know Mama," Harriet said with an affectionate smile. "She always makes light of her illness."

"Lady Carrbridge is much worse than she admits," the governess said. "I daresay this news will carry her off entirely."

"Thank you, Julia, but let us be optimistic," Harriet said crisply. "Will you ring for some brandy, if you please? Dev looks in great need of some fortification, and I am not averse myself."

"Not much of a lady's drink, brandy," the governess said sourly, but she rang the bell anyway.

Dev had never much liked Miss Laine, and liked her even less now. Harriet had long since outgrown the need for formal teaching, such as a governess might provide, yet here Miss Laine still was, clinging on like a barnacle to a ship's hull. A companion and chaperon she called herself now, but surely Harriet had aunts and cousins enough for that purpose.

The brandy arrived, Miss Laine poured a very small amount for each of them, taking her own glass without hesitation, despite her words of disapprobation. The brandy was warming, and after finishing the small amount offered in two mouthfuls and then refilling his glass, Dev began to feel better. There was nothing like brandy for putting a rosier glow on things.

"He will not really die, will he?" he said after a while. "He has always been so strong. Surely a little chill is not enough to carry him off."

"Dr Milligan has told me to prepare for the worst," Harriet said sombrely. "If he recovers... we must pray for such an outcome, naturally, but he is very bad, Dev, very bad indeed. This is more than a chill, for his heart is not behaving as it ought and could give out on him at any moment. He knows it, too. To send for you in that particular way... he has accepted his own departure, and is passing on the mantle to you as his heir. What did he say to you? Although if it was very private, pray say nothing about it."

"Not private, no. Only to take care of my brothers, because the sons of a marquess ought to be somebody."

"How peculiar," Miss Laine said with a sniff. "As if a lord is not somebody already."

"Then there was something about finding them careers because he had not got round to it himself. Which is odd, because none of them is old enough to be thinking of careers, as Father himself has insisted upon many times."

"So he did," Harriet said. "When Monty said something last summer about being a younger son and perhaps he might enter the church when he was old enough, Father said he was not to think about it, not for a very long time. *'Get yourself a decent education and then enjoy life for a few years, that is the proper way for the son of a marquess to go on. If you get bored when you are thirty or so, then you might think about a career.'* So I do not quite understand what he meant by saying he had not got round to it himself."

Dev took another long draught of brandy, feeling the mellowness seeping into his very bones. "I daresay it means nothing. The illness has addled his brain, I should think."

But even as he spoke, he felt sure that was not the case. His father was nothing if not astute, and no chill or misbehaving heart, however severe, could addle that sharp mind of his. The words were bewildering, but the brandy was having its effect and it was too much effort to puzzle out his father's meaning.

~~~~~

Despite his prediction, the eighth marquess did in fact linger past the dawn and on through the gloomy half-light of a rainy November day. However, long before the next dawn he had breathed his last, and the Earl of Deveron became at the age of twenty one the ninth Marquess of Carrbridge. He had been
~~~~~

Deveron, or Dev to his closest friends, for so many years that it was hard to think of himself by any other name.

Letters were sent forth with the dismal news, and a stream of carriages arrived over the following days, to disgorge Dev's white-faced brothers and an assortment of weeping aunts and cousins, and stern-faced uncles.

The aunts hugged Dev and left damp patches on his lapels, murmuring, "You poor boy!" or "Your poor mama!". The uncles patted him on the back and said gruffly, "Dreadful business, my boy, quite dreadful." None of this required much in the way of a response apart from the occasional word of gratitude or agreement. For what was there to say? A man had died and left an empty space in his family which was impossible to fill. Dev was the head of the family now, but he felt both inadequate to fill his father's shoes and entirely unprepared for the abrupt nature of the transition.

The funeral passed off in the doleful manner of all such events, and the relentless rain made it even more of an ordeal than usual. Afterwards, as the carriages returned to Drummoor from the Marford mausoleum, all the servants lined up in the rain to acknowledge the new marquess, to Dev's surprise.

"Is that necessary?" he murmured to the ladies awaiting the return of the funeral party in the entrance hall.

"Most certainly it is," Aunt Juliana told him sternly. "You must be aware of what is due to your consequence, Francis. You are a marquess now, and a peer of the realm. You must never forget it, nor must you allow the servants to treat you with less than the deference due to your position."

"Yes, aunt," he said meekly, but nevertheless he straightened his back and held his head a little higher. A marquess! It was a fine thing indeed, and much as he had loved and respected his father, he would not have been human if he had not taken secret pleasure at his elevation in rank.

For a few days, Drummoor seethed with relations near and distant, and Dev thought he had never seen so much black crepe and bombazine. Such an unforgiving colour, and poor Harriet looked quite dreadful in her mourning clothes, when she should be in white muslin like other girls of her age.

Dev's brothers kept up his spirits for a while, but one by one they disappeared, Reggie to Oxford and the younger ones back to school. Harriet vanished too, off to Harrogate to support Mama in her grief, for she was too ill to travel. At least she took the prune-faced Miss Laine with her. Then the aunts and uncles and cousins began to disappear, too. The aunts had taken it upon themselves to arrange a rota, whereby two or three of them were always about the place. Then, after a week or two, one would disappear and a different one would take her place. Supporting him in his grief, they called it, but since they only spoke to him in hushed whispers, as if he were ill, he soon tired of their company.

Dev's sole male companion was Mr Penicuik, the chaplain. He was very deferential, his head bobbing about on his long neck, as if he were trying to reduce his great height and not tower over Dev. Deferential, but not obsequious, for he seemed to regard it as his duty to offer Dev a great deal of unsolicited advice. "It is not my place to speak, my lord, but..."

he would say, followed by a long homily, ending with, "Naturally, you must act as you think best, my lord."

Mr Sharp, the agent, was there, too, but he lived out and never dined with the family, so he was of no account. The expensive lawyers who had dealt with the will had returned to London, but their juniors toiled back and forth with papers to be signed and documents to be read and moneys to be disbursed. Every day there seemed to be a mountain of work to be got through, whether for Mr Sharp and the management of the estate, or for the lawyers, until Dev's head was spinning.

Yet there was nothing to be done but endure it. Mourning was a damnable business, constraining a fellow in a thousand miserable ways. He could not ride or drive out in his curricle or go up to town to see his friends, for if he so much as suggested such a thing, Mr Penicuik's lugubrious face would become even longer, and he would twist his hands about in the most irritating manner.

"Of course, my lord, if you insist upon it," he would say, while shaking his head sorrowfully. "It is not for me to advise you, not a man in your exalted position, and I so humble. If you really feel it appropriate, you must indeed do as you wish and risk the censure of the world."

So naturally, it was impossible. Nor could he even accept invitations to dinner from kind-hearted neighbours, for Mr Penicuik became quite agitated at the idea. Dev felt sure that if his mama were there, she would smile and pat his hand and tell him that of course he must go, for it would do him a world of good to escape from Drummoor for a few hours. He felt it himself, the confinement, almost like being in prison. He would give anything for a change of scene, and someone to talk to who wore no black.

But he was a marquess now and must behave appropriately, and so he sat at home and was lonely and miserable and wretched.

2: A Dinner At Lake Cottage

Luckily, Dev was not to remain in isolation for very long. After a decently respectable period, his neighbours considered it proper to resume morning calls, and so a succession of carriages lurched along the two mile long drive to the doors of Drummoor, from which descended an assortment of matrons and unmarried daughters from thirty miles round about.

He knew what their objective was, naturally. As the heir to a marquessate, he had long since grown used to being the focus of intense speculation from families with marriageable daughters, and several young ladies in the neighbourhood had nurtured hopes, or so he had been told.

But his father had kept a wary eye on any female who ventured too close. Once, when a debutante at a London ball had dropped a handkerchief near him, a misfortune that could happen to anyone, and Dev had stooped to retrieve it for her, as a gentleman should manifestly do, and they had fallen into conversation, as was entirely natural under the circumstances, his father had gone into a towering rage, and sent the young lady away in tears. And Dev had heard afterwards that his father had gone to see *her* father and insisted that she be sent away, and so Dev had never seen her again. He was rather sorry about it, for she was pretty and nicely spoken and so very interested in him and all his trivial little doings. After that, he restricted himself to the ladies that his father told him were suitable, and very dull they were too, the daughters of dukes and marquesses and earls, neither pretty nor fun, and not in the least interested in Dev himself.

But neighbours could not be avoided, and even his father, who hated the formal social round, had said gloomily that one must receive them with apparent pleasure and exchange conversation with them, even those below the Marfords in rank, which was almost all of them. His mother, on the other hand, had loved receiving callers in the long-ago days when she had been in good health. Since she came from an untitled family herself, she had always been particularly kind to those below her own station.

Dev was more of his mother's opinion on the subject. They felt like friends, these people who had known him since he was a baby. They remembered the triumph of his first brace of partridge, the alarm when his frisky young hunter had baulked at a hedge and tossed him into a ditch, and the embarrassment when he had missed his steps and bumped his partner at his very first Drummoor ball. And even his early mistakes in the ballroom had not mattered because it was only Miss Mallory, the hoydenish girl who had taken turns with him to ride the children's fat little pony in the lower meadow, and had chased him up and down the long gallery, shrieking with laughter. Just because she had become a demure young lady and he had become a marquess did not mean that he could no longer enjoy her company.

So they came, these neighbours and friends, the Miss Ellesmeres, the Melthwaites and Frimbles, the Peacocks, the Mallorys and the Dunboroughs, to pay their respects and offer condolences, but also to bring a little sunshine into Dev's life. And if some of the young ladies eyed him rather consideringly, that was not unexpected. Some of his visitors even took it upon themselves to offer him advice upon the subject.

"Well, Lord Carrbridge," said Lady Frimble, her vast proportions squeezed onto a chair several sizes too small. "You will be under siege, I daresay. Every marriageable girl will be setting her cap at you. A marquess, and you little more than a boy, so there will be caps set at you, I make no doubt. However, you need have no fears about my girls." She waved a languid hand towards her unmarried daughters, sitting in a bored row in their matching ruby pelisses, like over-large robins. "No sensible man will have any of 'em and I don't expect you to, neither, so you've nothing to fear there. But you'll need to watch out. Every ambitious mama in the county will want you nicely rolled up before you go back to town, so be careful."

"Thank you, I shall indeed. How is Sir Richard?" he added hastily, and the conversation turned into easier channels.

Not all his visitors were so straightforward. Viscount Melthwaite seemed to talk in another language altogether, so that although Dev understood the words, he always felt as if there were some meaning to them which lay just beyond his grasp.

"You will want to keep your options open for a while, I daresay, Carrbridge," the Viscount said. "Not rush your horse, as it were. Take your time about it. Pace yourself. Nothing worse than going at a ditch too fast, if you understand me."

"Oh, quite," Dev said, without the least notion what he meant.

"Next time you are in town, look me up at the club — I am there most evenings. You have been elected, I take it?"

"Oh yes. Indeed I have."

"Good, good. Well, look me up, as I say, and I will help you set something up. Your father would have done it for you, no doubt, had he lived, poor chap. No point depending on your uncles. Ha! A sorry lot they are, if you will forgive me saying so, and that rackety cousin of yours is too much the other way, if you take my meaning. I should be happy to see you straight."

"Um... thank you, Melthwaite. Much obliged, I am sure."

"No trouble at all, I do assure you. Very happy to be of service, and you need someone about you who knows how these things should be done. Too easy to make a hash of it, you know."

Dev did not know at all, but he smiled and nodded and said everything that was proper, all the while feeling that some important element of the conversation was evading his understanding.

It was a relief, therefore, when Crabbe threw open the door. "Mrs Mallory, Miss Mallory, Miss Elinor Mallory."

The widowed Mrs Mallory and her daughters were the nearest neighbours to Drummoor, their cottage on the edge of High Mishcombe village being no more than two hundred yards away. While carriages toiled two miles further by road to the impressive arched entrance to the estate and another two miles winding back through the park to the house, the Mallory ladies could walk along the path in a matter of minutes and be enjoying their second cup of tea before the carriage occupants had even gained access to the house.

Dev rose to his feet with a genuine smile on his face. "Mrs Mallory, how delightful to see you. Miss Mallory. Miss Elinor. You are all well, I trust?"

"Perfectly well, thank you, my lord," Mrs Mallory said.

"I do hope the wind has lessened a little, for it was unpleasantly blustery earlier."

"It still blows strong, but we hardy three do not regard a little wind, my lord, and it is no distance from Lake Cottage to your front door across the park."

With these pleasantries observed, the three ladies disposed themselves on chairs, tea and cake were ordered and Dev settled down to some more sensible conversation. Since Mrs Mallory had kindly placed herself beside the Melthwaites, Dev was left with the two young ladies. The elder Miss Mallory was the very same who had chased him down the long gallery and was the victim of Dev's ineptitude in the ballroom, so he felt entirely at ease with her and she with him.

"You have made some changes to this room," she said, looking about her with lively interest.

"Oh — really? I had not noticed. It was cleared out in the spring, when all the curtains and chandeliers were taken down, so I suppose everything was muddled up when the furniture was brought back in."

"Oh no, it is not muddled up, everything is just as it was, except that there was a very nice chess table just over there, by that cabinet, and two chairs beside it. Now it has gone and the chairs too, and everything has been moved about to fill the space, and this sofa was in that corner over there."

"How very observant you are," Dev said, not quite knowing what to say.

"Oh, but I know these rooms as well as I know ours at home." She smiled at him in a companionable way. "I should not forget them just because I have not been here for a few months. And how is your mama? No worse, I hope? She was wise not to come rushing home, for the journey would have quite overset her."

It was so easy to talk to Beatrice — she was so sensible, so understanding. There were no studied airs with her, for she said what she thought, although with the greatest delicacy. She was not a great beauty, and her own mother had been heard to describe her as homely, but she was kind and gentle, and Dev was at ease with her in a way he seldom enjoyed with any young lady. Certainly not with the grand ladies of the ton, who smiled and simpered at him, but whispered behind their fans as he passed by. He thought there was calculation in their eyes, whereas Beatrice was not in the least calculating. There were those who called her a schemer, but that business with Arthur Frimble had been just a misunderstanding, he was sure. Beatrice was too straightforward a person to scheme.

She had never had the good fortune of a season in London, for it was quite beyond her mother's means. Dev suspected there would be no money to settle on her, so there was no hope of a grand marriage, but he had always imagined that she would one day catch the eye of a parson with a comfortable living, or perhaps a lawyer in York. Or maybe she was romantically waiting for true love to smite her, although she seemed too sensible for such notions. He wished her well, but she was past twenty now and her chances of making a respectable match diminished every year.

The younger sister, however, was another matter. Elinor was the pretty one, although she was dreadfully bookish which would be enough to put any man off. Still, she was but sixteen, and in a year or two would no doubt be breaking hearts all over the county.

"And how are you, Dev?" Beatrice said. "Are you very miserable? Naturally you are. What a dreadful business. I was devastated when Papa died, but of course we had to move out of the Hall at once, so there was no time to repine. It helped, I believe, to be in a new place, with no memories to distress us. But here, every room must remind you of your father, and the weight of your lineage bearing down on you. He was such a great man, a great leader of his people. He will be sorely missed by the whole nation. You must be wondering how you can possibly follow in his commanding footsteps."

Dev was much struck by this speech, so much in sympathy with his own feelings. How was he ever to cope with the duties and responsibilities that now fell to him? He had barely cast off the trappings of childhood, and felt wholly inadequate to assume the mantle of a peer of the realm. He was nought but a boy, and his father had been as far above him as the moon. To be sure, he had never himself seen his father as a great leader, more as a somewhat brusque parent, often absent, and querulous if his morning chocolate was not just as he liked it. However, he had heard of his father's famous orations in the House of Lords, and the times when his words had tipped the balance in the voting for an important bill.

Beatrice was not dismayed by Dev's silence, for she went on, "How you must be rattling round in this place, with everyone away, and no amusements to while away the days. Are you quite dreadfully bored?"

"It is true, the place is very quiet, and there is not even a tolerable game of billiards to be had, when even Hatty is away."

"Why, then, you must dine with us one evening," she said firmly. "It will do you good."

Dev's spirits soared — an evening with the Mallory ladies would be just the thing to cheer him up. But was it proper? "I do not think Mr Penicuik would approve," he said dolefully.

"Why ever should he not? It would only be a family dinner, you know, nothing formal. I am sure there could not be the least objection. I will suggest it to Mama."

Mrs Mallory took her daughter's view of the matter, the invitation was issued and promptly accepted, and to Lake Cottage therefore he was to go.

~~~~~

Lake Cottage was a pleasant house which could have fitted comfortably into the grand saloon at Drummoor, with room to spare. The house had been given its name because of the distant views of Mishmere from the upper windows, although Beatrice liked to joke that it was because in wet weather the garden itself became a lake. Dev was glad he had chosen to take the carriage to his dinner engagement, rather than try to hop between the puddles.

He had been there many times before, and had always liked the place. Sometimes the sheer size of Drummoor lowered his spirits, especially in his father's writing room, where his grandfather glowered down from a larger-than-life portrait on one wall. Everything about the place was larger than life, and made him feel like a mouse creeping about the endless corridors or scuttling through the saloons. Lake Cottage was a proper size for humans, cosy and intimate and friendly. He always felt at home there.

Mrs Mallory had invited the village clergyman and his wife, as well as the local apothecary, and Mr Penicuik to make up the numbers and provide some gentlemen to share the port with Dev. He did not mind, for they were all well known to him. Parson and Mrs Spiller were a couple in their middle years, each as stout as the other. With their children grown and gone, their mission in life was to collect samples of every flower that grew wild in the fields and hedgerows round about, each to be dried and pressed and described in the
~~~~~

minutest detail for a great work that they hoped to have published one day. The apothecary, Mr Dunshaw, was a widower with two small boys who had the clear intent of making Elinor the second Mrs Dunshaw.

So it was that eight sat down to dinner in Mrs Mallory's dining room, being four gentlemen and four ladies, creating a most pleasing symmetry, and the dinner was just as pleasing, even though there was only one course. Dev sat at Mrs Mallory's right hand, with Beatrice on his other side. As Mrs Mallory was much occupied in conversation with the apothecary to her left, and Mr Spiller held the attention of the rest of the table, Dev had the pleasure of talking uninterruptedly to Beatrice.

"Shall you make any changes at Drummoor now that you are in control of the estate, Dev?"

"I had not thought about it. Mama..."

"Of course. You will want to consult Lady Carrbridge. A female view on such matters is always essential, I feel. Still, it may be spring before the roads are fit for her to travel in her state of health, so it is as well to be thinking of such things early, and such a project would be just the thing to keep you busy and forget your sad bereavement. There are some improvements that could be made to the pleasure grounds, but that would have to wait for the better weather, I fear. What about the interior? The saloons are looking a little faded, do you not think? Some new wallpaper, perhaps in the Chinese manner, and a few pieces of more stylish furniture would make all the difference, do you not agree?"

"I am not sure that I want to change anything," he said, twirling his wine glass absently. "There is so much history in those rooms."

"Exactly!" she said. "Everywhere one sees the hand of your predecessors. Every painting, every urn, every chair was chosen by some other person. Naturally you will want to make your mark on the house, to make it your own. Otherwise, it will be as if nothing has changed, and no one will respect you as they ought. You will merely be in your father's shadow, when you should step forward to take your rightful place in the sun."

"Oh, that is very poetic," he said, seeing the full force of this point of view. "I do believe you are right, although — Ah, thank you, Mrs Mallory, a little more beef would be most acceptable. Thank you, it is delicious. As I say, Beatrice, you are right, but I should not know where to begin."

"Oh, with the grand saloon, I should suggest." She sipped her wine thoughtfully. "Or perhaps that is too large a project to begin with. The music room might be a better choice. It is a very nondescript room at the moment, with all those pale colours and the plasterwork so plain! It needs something more appropriate to your position in society for those occasions when you hold recitals there. Plenty of gold trim, I should suggest, and stronger colours, with some statuary to enliven the walls and the ceiling painted with nymphs and the like."

"That sounds... very striking," he murmured, not quite able to envisage it, or imagine why he might hold recitals. "Nymphs..."

"Something classical, anyway," she said, laughing. "It need not be nymphs precisely. Should you like me to show you what I mean, next time I visit Drummoor? It would be easier to describe if we were to be in the room itself."

"That would be very kind of you, Beatrice," he said. Such a helpful person, and a good friend to him, always thinking of his comfort. As the ladies withdrew, and he watched her shapely figure leave the room, he found himself thinking of her most complacently.

3: Winter

To Dev's surprise, Beatrice arrived shortly after breakfast. He was not unhappy to see her, for her arrival called him away from a tedious meeting with Sharp, the agent. Meetings with Sharp were always tedious, for Dev had no head for business in the slightest, and his father had always said kindly, "Never mind, my boy, it will all make sense when you are older, and if not, Sharp is very capable, very capable indeed. You can leave all to him."

Dev would have been perfectly willing to leave all to Sharp, but the wretched man believed it to be his duty to explain every detail of the estate: the tenant farmers, the minor estates, the income from wood and wool and grain, the mills and smithies and cottages whose occupants owed allegiance to their lord in a positively feudal manner. Yet if he ever got impatient and asked the agent to skip over the details and just tell him what his income was, the man shook his head sorrowfully. "Ah, my lord, if only it were so simple!"

Never was there a more miserable specimen of humanity than Sharp, with his long face and melancholy demeanour, his long-winded descriptions of places Dev had never even heard of before. Had his father understood any of this? Had he been able to hold a sensible conversation about wool? If so, Dev had never observed it, or heard him mention wool at all except in reference to a new coat. Perhaps he himself had left the agent to manage everything. For all Sharp's lugubrious expression and badly-made coats, the man seemed to know his business.

Beatrice, by contrast, was a refreshing picture in a charmingly fashioned pelisse and a very stylish bonnet, which framed her features in the most pleasing way. She was no beauty, but with her complexion heightened by the walk across the park, she looked very well, and his smile of greeting was not entirely due to relief from escaping Mr Sharp's teachings.

"Beatrice! How delightful to see you so early. But there is nothing wrong, I hope? Your mama? Elinor?"

"No, no, nothing in the world, but they are too busy today to accompany me and I could not wait to explain to you all my ideas for the music room. You are not going to be stuffy about propriety, are you? We are such old friends, are we not?"

"The music room? Oh, the music room! Of course. Yes, we need not stand upon ceremony, I am sure. Let us go there at once. Crabbe, a fire in the music room if you please."

While a footman wrestled with the fire, and another brought tea and cakes, and then a bottle of something more fortifying for Dev, and while Mrs Compton, the housekeeper, hovered nervously in case Miss Mallory should find any deficiency in her housemaids' work, Beatrice herself strode about the room, arms gesturing widely. Dev still could not quite see in his mind just how the room might look if all these grandiose schemes were to come to fruition. Still, he understood the salient points — that the room was very plain and drab as it stood, that refurbishment was needed and that Beatrice was just the person to order such refurbishment.

She left him with his head spinning, filled with so many ideas that he feared it might explode. The following day she came again, this time with her sketchpad to show him her ideas set to paper. The day after, she brought a journal which showed the exact style of pianoforte which she thought best suited to the size and shape of the room. The next day was Sunday, but on Monday she was there again, with some samples of a possible wallpaper. And if he thought it a little odd that she came so often, and sometimes without even her mama or sister as chaperon, he explained it as an exuberance of enthusiasm for the project, and perfectly acceptable in such an old friend.

And in this pleasant way, the final days of autumn drifted away.

~~~~~

Christmas filled Drummoor with noise and laughter and music and excellent company, mourning or no. Dev's brothers emerged from their academic establishments, and Harriet returned from Harrogate, bringing the sour-faced Miss Laine and the disheartening news that Mama was still too ill to travel and would now see out the winter in her comfortable
~~~~~

hotel. She had found a good doctor there, who advised rest and a new dietary regime, so she was optimistic of an improvement soon. She sent a long letter to Dev, reminding him that he had been trained all his life for the rank he now held, so he must not be afraid of it. He felt excessively untrained, but the thought was kind. His mother always made him feel better, somehow.

Besides the immediate family, vast numbers of aunts and uncles and cousins and other more distant kin descended on Drummoor for a month of good food and good wine and good company, and plenty of all three. They could not attend the more formal local events because of their mourning, but they were a large enough party to form their own card evening, or put together a play or even an impromptu dance. The entertainment extended into less restrained areas, too. The feud between Aunt Agnes and Aunt Patience moved into its seventeenth year. Another urn in the long gallery was overturned in mysterious circumstances. Another footman was hastily turned off after an incident with a visiting lady's maid. And another gentlemanly boxing bout ended with Gil and several of the cousins rolling on the floor in a violent wrestling match, although no bones were broken this time, and the damage to furniture was slight.

Dev had to endure a great many lectures from various uncles, individually or in groups, who saw it as their sacred duty to watch over their fatherless nephew, and oversee his emergence into society in his full glory as a marquess.

"You will want to take your seat sooner rather than later," Uncle Ambrose said. "Who will introduce you? Oh, Camberley, I suppose. He was an old friend of your father."

"Or Dunmorton," Uncle Jacob said, his reedy voice quavering. "Very well in with everyone, Dunmorton is."

"Very well in with the Whigs, you mean," Uncle Joshua said in disgust. "You will want to have as little as possible to do with anything of that nature, Francis. Not at all the thing."

"Oh no, uncle," he said hastily. "We have always been Tory, have we not? No thought of switching horses now."

"Quite right, quite right," boomed Uncle Thomas, an amply endowed gentleman with chins which wobbled whenever he spoke. "Indeed, best to keep out of politics altogether. No point complicating your life by trying to form an opinion on matters of that nature. It only addles the brain, or so I have found. Leave it to wiser heads. Take your seat, make your maiden speech, of course, but you need only say the usual things — duty to the country and the king and so forth. Then keep out of it unless you are told to vote. Much the best way."

They all nodded sagely.

"Camberley, then," Uncle Ambrose said.

"Or Dunmorton..."

"No, Jacob, I believe it will have to be Camberley, but there is no rush, no rush at all. Let the boy catch his breath, eh?"

Dev smiled and agreed with everything that was said, letting the conversation drift around him like smoke. It seemed to have nothing to do with him, all this talk of the House of Lords and speeches and duty to the country. That was his father, not him. And when they had all wandered away and left him alone, he could never remember a word that had been said, and allowed his thoughts to revert to wallpaper samples and sketches and the proper place for a pianoforte, and the animated countenance of a certain young lady.

It was not long before Beatrice's sketches and samples were discovered, when a group of the younger family members had retreated to the music room, ostensibly to practise duets for a performance, but in reality to escape the watchful eyes of the aunts.

"Whose drawings are these?" Harriet said, picking up the sketch book. "Oh, is it meant to be this room? Prettily accomplished. And wallpaper samples. Dev, are you planning some improvements without telling us?"

"Oh, not really," he said airily. "But Beatrice thought—"

"*Beatrice?* What is it to her? Oh Dev, are you sweet on her? For that will never do, you know, not Beatrice Mallory. She has not a penny to her name, and for all she has nice manners, she is not a fit wife for a marquess."

"Good Lord, no, it is nothing of the sort," he said at once, horrified. "What do you take me for? I have known her for ever, Hatty. Why, we practically grew up together. I have no idea of marrying her."

"Thank goodness, because it would distress Mama so if you were to throw yourself away on someone like that. I have nothing against her, you understand, for she is a very good sort of girl and I wish her a splendid husband, just so long as it is not you."

"Not the least thought of marriage, I do assure you."

"Good," Harriet said. "You do not need to think about such things for years yet. Nor refurbishments, either. If there is anything that needs doing, it is for Mama to determine, do you not agree? She is still mistress of this house, after all."

"But of course. I had no intention... No actual plans, not as such... It was just..."

"She just wanted to give you a distraction, I daresay, to stop you moping about the place," Harriet said. "She is a kind girl, Beatrice, and I am sure she meant it for the best. But you will tell her it is out of the question, will you not?"

"Naturally I shall."

"Good. Julia, have you not found the music yet? How difficult can it be?"

~~~~~

January saw the gradual departure of most of the gathering. One or two of the unmarried aunts lingered on, having no particular place to be until the season opened in London, and happy to have the comfort of plentiful coal, a good dinner every night and enough servants to meet every need, none of which they need pay for out of their own pockets. But as they never left their bedrooms before two or three in the afternoon, and dozed away the evenings, Dev hardly noticed they were there.

Mr Sharp's instruction in the management of the estate had been reduced to a mere once a week irritation, and Dev was more than ever at a loose end. Now that the first two months of mourning had passed, he ventured to write to
~~~~~

some of his university friends to come and bear him company. His approaches were unfruitful, for they were all unable to come, whether snowed up in Northumberland, bogged down in Cornwall, ill with an array of fevers and spots and other malaises, or dancing attendance on relatives.

"And I suppose as soon as the weather or their health improves, they will be off to town for the season, and I suppose I cannot go?" he said gloomily to Mr Penicuik one morning at breakfast.

"You would surely not wish to be gadding about at parties with your dear papa so lately gone from this mortal plane?" Penicuik said, his head bobbing about on its long neck. Below it, Dev had to avert his eyes from such a badly tied cravat.

"No, indeed, but a change of scene would do me a great deal of good, I believe."

"You might ask Mr Sharp to allow you to accompany him on his next round of visits to the northern parts of your holdings, Lord Carrbridge," Penicuik said. "It would be instructive as well as a diversion, and I am convinced that your tenants would be delighted by your interest."

Since a journey with Mr Sharp was quite the least pleasurable diversion Dev could conceive of, he made no answer.

It was fortunate that the Mallory ladies were so assiduous in their visits, for Dev would have been in a sad way without their company on an almost daily basis, enlivened by the addition of their twelve-year-old brother Edmund, who was staying with them for the present. He had been adopted by a wealthy uncle with no heirs, and was being raised by him in York. Just before Christmas, however, the boy had developed some putrid fever, with a great profusion of spots, and the old man, fearing for his own health, had sent Edmund back to his mother until he should be to a certainty free from all risk of contagion.

The ladies were delighted to have the child with them for the first time in many years, and Dev was just as pleased. Edmund reminded him very much of his own younger brothers — indeed, he was the same age as Monty — so he was happy to spend hours showing the boy around the more interesting corners of Drummoor, and playing childish games with him in the old nursery.

On one occasion, the two of them were engrossed in a game of spillikins with Beatrice and Elinor.

"Dev, have you thought any more on the changes we discussed for the music room? For there is a man in York who—"

"Cannot be done, I am afraid," he said absently.

"Oh." There was a long silence, then, "Not at all?"

"Not the least possibility."

"Oh. You do not like my ideas?"

He looked up from the game, detecting some change in her tone. Was she angry with him? "I like your ideas very well, and if it were all up to me I should not hesitate, but Hatty pointed out that Mama is the mistress of the house, and it is for her to decide on such matters."

"Is it?" Beatrice said, her tone as mild as milk now. "Naturally Lady Carrbridge is the mistress of Drummoor, and far be it from me to undermine her authority, but *you* are the master here now, Dev. It is for you to make all the important decisions."

He licked his lips, not knowing how to reply. He had quite enjoyed Beatrice's visits and the fun of having a shared project to talk about, but he had never particularly wanted to make any changes to the music room. It had been a relief, in a way, when Harriet had told him to leave it to Mama. It felt like the right thing to do, to pass all such decisions to the one person who had always taken them. Who was more capable than Mama, and who knew better what was right for Drummoor?

Now he felt trapped, as if it would be a weakness, almost an abdication of duty, to hand the job over to Mama. He licked his lips again.

"You are too timid, sometimes, Dev," Beatrice said, laughter in her eyes. "You are a marquess now, you know, and you must learn to assert your authority."

He was stung by this accusation. Too timid? He would show her how well he could exert his authority. "You forget yourself, Beatrice," he said in his haughtiest voice. "Do not tell me how to behave."

She coloured, and looked down at her hands in her lap. "I beg your pardon, Lord Carrbridge. I did not mean to presume, only to speak as a friend of many years."

"Well now, never mind," he said gruffly. "It shall be forgotten. As for the music room, there is no need to rush into anything. You may show your ideas to Mama when she returns home."

"Thank you, I shall do so," she said demurely, and they returned to the game as if nothing had happened, and by the time the Lake Cottage family had departed, Dev was quite in charity with Beatrice again.

4: Rumours

A spell of drier weather enabled Dev to walk to the village occasionally. He had no particular business to attend to there, but being cooped up in the house with no company but Mr Penicuik and the aunts was driving him wild, and riding about the countryside was a solitary pursuit. What he needed was someone to talk to, and if he walked down the main street and bought one or two small items from the shops there, he would be sure to meet some of his acquaintance along the way.

Or so he thought, but Mishcombe was not a large village, nor were its attractions sufficient to bring onto the streets anyone Dev might talk to. The gentry of Mishcombe were, it appeared, tucked away in their parlours, toes to the fire. The only people he met were the lower orders, the farmers and shoemakers and ironmongers and their wives, who made him the usual obeisances but were not people he could exchange more than a few words with, if that.

But his journey took him past Lake Cottage, and there, he knew, he might always find a welcome. So it was that on days when Beatrice failed to walk to Drummoor, Dev would happen to walk into the village and feel obliged, as a courtesy, to call. The ladies plied him with tea and cakes and entertained him so well that he often stayed more than an hour in the pretty drawing room, so feminine with its floral wallpaper and delicate china ornaments.

One day, he met Mrs Spiller, the clergyman's wife, in the grocer's shop.

"Oh, Lord Carrbridge, how delightful!" she began. "We have all been talking about you, as I am sure you are aware."

This was not unusual, for the village gossipped relentlessly about its noble neighbours, so Dev smiled. "How flattering," he murmured.

"Oh, yes, so exciting! We are all so pleased. Oh, but perhaps I should not have mentioned it." Her hand flew to her mouth in alarm. "Is it a great secret?"

"Secret?" he said, floundering. "What secret?"

"Why, you and Miss Mallory of course! So happy for you both."

"Miss Mallory? What is this about Miss Mallory?"

"Oh, you men!" She tapped him playfully on one arm. "You like to pretend there is nothing going on, as if you are nought but friends, so that you may surprise everyone later."

"I do not in the least like pretence of any sort," he said.

"Not to worry, your secret is safe with me," she trilled.

"I do assure you, madam, there is no secret."

She tipped her head on one side, the feathers in her hat bouncing, and frowned. "Truly? No secret? Then you and Miss Mallory...? There is no...?"

"No, indeed!" He laughed at her foolish mistake. "Beatrice is a good friend, but there is nothing more between us, I do assure you. Why, we have known each other for ever, quite like brother and sister."

"Oh. I see. Nothing?"

"You must believe me, madam, when I say that there is no romantic attachment between myself and Miss Mallory. The very idea is—" He was about to say *'ridiculous'* when he recollected that this was not very flattering to Beatrice. "It is impossible."

For a moment she eyed him uncertainly, but then heaved a great sigh. "What a pity! Such a charming idea, and we should all have liked it excessively."

"It is a puzzle to me how such rumours ever get started, when there is not the least foundation for them," he said. "But it is a good joke — Miss Mallory and me! So very diverting. I shall tell Beatrice all about it when next I see her, for she will enjoy it very much."

"Oh — do you think so? But young ladies do not always find it amusing to hear their names bandied about in hearsay, Lord Carrbridge."

"Then you think perhaps I should not mention it?"

"It would be best to say nothing, I believe. I daresay the story only arose because you have been seen visiting Lake Cottage once or twice lately. You know how people's minds work — a gentleman has only to visit a second time in a week, or stay longer than the usual half-hour, and the gossips get to work."

"Indeed. Some people have nothing better to do than spread scurrilous rumours," he said indignantly.

She smiled and nodded, and they parted amicably.

Dev walked home in thoughtful mood, for it occurred to him that if these rumours should be widespread, it might expose Beatrice to ridicule as a woman with disappointed hopes. He knew that she had no such hopes, but the world saw only what it wanted to see — a young, unmarried woman who was friendly with a marquess. Naturally there would be those making an incorrect reading of the circumstances. Beatrice was already beyond the first freshness of youth, and he had no wish to blight her already slim chances of securing a husband of her own class. As he came to Lake Cottage, he looked wistfully at its latticed windows and the faint glow of a lamp within, but then resolutely passed by.

~~~~~

Two days later, Beatrice arrived at Drummoor, alone.

"Are you avoiding us, Dev?" she said, with her easy smile.

"Not at all. I have been busy, that is all."

"It must be important indeed to keep you from our door," she said teasingly.

"I have been working through some of Father's papers," he said. "Not that I understand them above half, but I have to do it."
~~~~~

"Maybe I can help," she said. "Should you like me to give you a hand? I am very good at sorting papers. I always kept the accounts for Papa, you know, and after he died the attorney said everything was in perfect order."

Appealing as the prospect of congenial company was during such a dull task, he knew he could not accept it. "Not really appropriate, Beatrice. Private papers and so forth. Personal business." He felt himself colouring as he spoke and could only hope that Beatrice would take the hint and drop the subject.

"Personal business? Like a journal or some such? No, that would not be appropriate. But other papers—"

"No, Beatrice," he said firmly.

"Oh." They were still standing in the entrance hall, Crabbe and two footmen waiting impassively for any instructions. She looked about her, as if for inspiration. "There must be something I can do to help you."

"Come into the saloon," he said.

"What about the library?" she said, turning to him gleefully. "There is plenty of work for willing hands *there,* I fancy."

"Work? In the library? What possible work can there be?"

"Oh, sorting the books," she said vaguely.

"*Sorting* them?" he said bewildered. "Whatever for?"

"Why, to put them in a proper order, of course," she said. "Come on, let me show you."

The library was freezing. Crabbe, following behind them, said, "Should you like the fires lit, my lord?"

"We shall not be here long enough, Crabbe. Miss Mallory is only going to show me something."

"Very good, my lord." Crabbe withdrew, but he left the doors wide open.

"Better make this quick, Beatrice," Dev said, blowing on his hands. "It is colder than a tomb in here. Look, I can see my breath, that is how cold it is. I shall need my greatcoat if we stay here long."

"Nonsense!" she said. "What a feeble creature you are, sometimes, Dev. A little cold never hurt anyone. Look, here is what I mean. The books in this cabinet are quite a jumble, all mixed up. They need sorting."

"But they *are* sorted," he cried. "The tallest ones are on this shelf and the smallest ones are at the top there. See?"

"That is not sorting, silly boy! They need to be arranged in alphabetical order."

"But why?"

"So that you might be able to find the book you want to read, of course."

"Oh, no one ever reads them, Beatrice. I like them as they are."

She laughed. "Well, *I* should like to read them."

"It is very dull stuff, I do assure you — sermons and philosophical treatises and travel books, nothing at all interesting."

"I should very much like to read a travel book. Do you have anything on Italy?"

"Well…" He spun round, looking at the endless cabinets, all filled with books, as if a volume on Italy might suddenly appear. "The travel books are over here," he said, leading her across the room to a corner near the window and opening the cabinet. "But I do not know which are about Italy."

"I cannot see any. There is one up there which is about Paris. That might be interesting. I am not sure if I can reach it."

She stood on the tips of her toes and reached up.

"Wait, wait, let me," Dev said, rushing forward.

And somehow, he was not quite sure how it happened, Beatrice fell back just as he reached her and there she was in his arms, warm and heavy and laughing up at him.

"Oh, Dev," she said, smiling at him in such a way that he was hot and excited and half-delirious all at once, as if he were drunk or in a feverish dream.

When she reached up and pulled his head towards her, he made no protest and kissed her soundly.

It seemed a long time before their lips parted. Dev had no wish for them to be parted at all, indeed he felt that he could kiss Beatrice all day, but he felt vaguely that he ought not to. He was not quite sure why, for it was very pleasant — very pleasant indeed! — and Beatrice was perfectly amenable, but some instinct made him draw back.

"Oh, Dev!" she giggled, blushing. "I am all astonishment! You quite take me by surprise."

This was a bit rich, considering that she had initiated the kiss, but he did not quite like to contradict a lady. Besides, he found himself a little short of breath just then.

"Book?" was all he could manage to say.

She stared at him, her brows snapping together.

"You wanted a book, I believe." He scanned the shelves. "Ah, this one on Paris." He reached up and pulled it down.

"Really, Dev, how can you think about books at such a time?"

"But you were the one who wanted it," he said. "Have you changed your mind now?"

For an instant, she looked so angry that he thought she was about to explode. Then, quite abruptly, her expression shifted and she tittered. "The book, of course. You quite put it out of my head. May I borrow it? I shall take the greatest care of it, I assure you."

"Of course you may, for no one else reads any of these. Well, Gus and Monty, perhaps, if they have nothing else to do. Oh, look! Here is one about Italy after all. I wonder why we did not see it before?"

And so the awkward moment passed. Dev gathered up the books she had chosen — she found three to her liking in the end — and saw her to the front door as she set off on the short walk home. But he was left with the vague feeling that he had done something wrong, and the memory of that kiss, pleasurable as it had been, was not as satisfying as it ought to have been.

~~~~~
~~~~~

The next day brought a long letter from Mama. Her missives were always a delight to read, for in some unfathomable way she made Dev feel that, no matter what had gone wrong, all would be well and he was not so foolish and unworldly as he often felt himself to be. This letter was different.

'My dearest boy, Reports have reached me of a most alarming nature. I am sure there can be no truth in them, but I must put you on your guard so that you may do nothing to give rise to any ill-informed speculation or excite expectation in the wrong quarter. It is being said that there is an understanding between you and Beatrice Mallory. My first thought was that this is mere rumour, based on nothing more than your long stay at Drummoor, coupled with her family's proximity. On rereading your recent letters, however, I see now that you have indeed been spending a great deal of time in her company. Francis, you must be very careful. Beatrice is a pleasant enough girl, but I should not like to see her installed as mistress of Drummoor. I am not, as you know, one of those matchmaking mamas who insists her eldest must choose a wife by rank alone, but there must be some consideration of suitability, and the great disparity of rank, fortune and situation between the two of you would render the match most unwise. That would not weigh with me were I to be convinced of your mutual affection, but I do not find any sign of such in your manner of writing of her. As for Beatrice herself, I cannot say what she may feel for you, but I do know that your dear papa warned her away from you, or any of the boys, only two years ago. I should be disappointed if your affections were to turn in that direction. I know I can depend on you to be sensible, Francis. One day you will meet a young lady who entrances you so thoroughly that you will want to

marry her more than anything in the world, and she you, but I pray that day will not be too soon. Until then, you must be on your guard. You are extremely eligible, especially now that you have the title and full control of your fortune and are old enough to marry without my permission, and many a young woman will try to entice you to fall in love with her. It is a comfort to me to know that you are wise enough to see through such stratagems, and strong enough to resist every ploy. I depend upon your good sense. Your loving Mama.'

This letter agitated Dev so much that he could not bear to be still. Despite a light rain, he sent for his horse and rode up onto the moors to gallop away his nerves and forget for a time his disordered thoughts. It was only when he noticed a coating of snow on his horse's mane that he turned back, riding home more cautiously in the afternoon's waning light.

That word haunted him: *'disappointed'*. There was nothing in the world so awful as a disappointed parent. His father had been disappointed in him more than once, but he had, he hoped, grown out of the worst of his mistakes, and had not incurred his father's disapprobation for some years now. But his mother! She had never yet expressed her disappointment in him, and the very thought of it wrenched at him in the most painful way. No, he must not disappoint his mother, who had always had such faith in him.

As he rode slowly home, heedless of his surroundings, there was some comfort in the recollection that he had not, in fact, made any commitment to Beatrice. He had never spoken of love or offered for her or suggested in any way by his actions that he thought of her other than as a friend. The memory of their kiss prickled his conscience, for surely kisses were for lovers? He did not feel like a lover. He held Beatrice in affection, certainly, but not in that way. Certainly not in that way. The kiss had just happened, exactly as one might offer a hand to assist a lady over a stile, or lift her down from her horse, and nothing was to be inferred from the contact. It was not as if he had intended it, or taken her into the library alone so that he might kiss her. No, his conscience was clear on that point.

But still it niggled at him that these rumours had reached even Harrogate to disturb his mama, and raise the awful prospect of disappointment.

~~~~~

Two days later, Beatrice returned with the books.

"These were very interesting. May I borrow some more?" she said, as she was shown into the drawing room, where Dev was reading a newspaper.

"Of course. Do help yourself. The cabinets are not locked."

"How shall I reach the higher shelves?"

"There is a ladder," he said, absently. "All libraries have a ladder for the purpose."

"You are not very chivalrous, Dev," she said, laughing. "Come and help me, do, for you can reach the high books much more easily than I can."

He looked up then, and, with an answering smile, folded his newspaper and set it down on a side table. "Very well, Miss Mallory, I shall be chivalrous and reach the books for you. Or perhaps I will hold the ladder while you reach them."
~~~~~

"How silly you are, Dev! Come along."

She tucked one arm into his in a way that made him feel a little uncomfortable, but he did not like to object to such intimacy, for surely nothing that Beatrice did could be improper. But when they reached the library, she closed the doors firmly, and that he could not agree to.

"No, we must leave the doors open, Beatrice. For propriety, and so forth."

"Propriety? What does that matter now? Kiss me again, Dev." And she advanced on him with a determined look on her face.

"No, no!" he said, backing away from her in haste. "We should not..."

He bumped into a bookcase, and could go no further, but still she advanced, arms reaching for him. He slipped out of her grasp, and strode away down the room. She followed, and he half-ran to put a low cabinet between them. As she moved one way, he moved the other.

"Stop this, Beatrice!"

She faced him across the cabinet, her eyes wide and for a moment he was terrified that she might cry.

"What is the matter with you?" she cried. "Why should we not kiss? After all, we are as good as engaged!"

5: A Question Of Honour

Dev was too stupefied to answer. Engaged? How could she possibly think so? One kiss was not any kind of offer of marriage.

"It is unkind in you to tease me like this," she went on.

His mouth flapped open like a fish, and he could not string two words into a coherent order.

"Did it mean nothing to you when you kissed me?" she said. "Were you taking advantage of my innocence? Now you have damaged my reputation and—"

That startled a response from him. "I have done no such thing! Good Lord, Beatrice, what has got into you?"

"But you kissed me!" she said, eyes narrowed. "What else am I supposed to think? You should not have done it if you did not intend to marry me."

"You fell into my arms!" he said indignantly. "And *you* kissed *me*, if I recall correctly. Really, Beatrice, if you think a man must marry a girl just because he has kissed her, then bats must have got into your head. It takes more than that to wreck a girl's reputation, you know."

She flushed crimson. "So you are backing out of it now, are you? I might have known you would not honour your promise."

"I made you no promises, none at all, and you cannot argue that I did."

"But you implied it when you kissed me, Dev. That is as good as an engagement."

"Nonsense! I have not even offered for you!"

"Then you had better get on with it, if you are a man of honour."

Dev had no answer to her. What could he say? He knew the code of conduct expected of a man of his class, and he knew perfectly well that there was an element of truth in her arguments. A man who kissed a girl, even when the girl encouraged the kiss rather, might arouse expectations in her that only marriage could fulfil.

And yet every instinct rebelled. He had accorded her the intimacy of friendship, as one who had been a childhood playmate, and if she had read something more into that, the mistake was hers. Any marriage between them was out of the question, surely she could see that?

Yet there she stood, waiting for him to offer for her.

While he stood in an agony of indecision, trying to find an escape from his dilemma, voices could be heard in the distance, Crabbe's low murmur and a loud, masculine voice, one that was very familiar.

"Humphrey?" he said, bewildered, for his brother was supposed to be at school.

Moments later, booted feet rat-tat-tatted to the library door and knocked sharply on it. "Not interrupting anything, am I?" A blond head appeared, grinning mischievously. "What a cosy little scene. How are you, Beatrice? Well, I trust?"

"Perfectly, I thank you, Humphrey. I was just leaving. Dev, we will discuss this another time."

So saying, she swept out, head high.

Dev collapsed into the nearest chair. "Good God, Humph, you cannot imagine how glad I am to see you. I am in the most dreadful coil— Wait, what are you doing here? It is not Easter already?"

Humphrey laughed, and hurled himself into a matching chair. He was a solid, fair-haired young man, already taller than Dev, and twice his width, for he was an enthusiastic boxer who had never yet been bested.

"I have been rusticated again."

"Oh, Humph, not dog fights again?"

"No, no, this was far more fun," he said, eyes gleaming with merriment. "You remember Miss Watson?"

"The spinster sister of that fusty history master?"

"The very same. Well, a few of the fellows got up a game with her. Stoner started it — he is up for anything, such a bang-up fellow. He put up a monkey, and then everyone joined in, betting which of them would be the first to kiss her."

"What?" Dev said. "Why, she must be forty if she is a day! And a face like the back of a cow."

"She is thirty three, but I will concede to the accuracy of your description of her face."

"Tell me you did not kiss her! Even for a bet, I should not want to do it."

"Lord, no, I just kept the book. But Ramsey was in on it, and Stoner and... well, several others you would not know, I daresay. We have all been rusticated, but it hardly signifies, since it is almost time for the Easter recess. But what is going on here? Tell me about this coil you are in. I hope it has nothing to do with Beatrice."

"Why do you say that?" Dev said cautiously.

"Because she is a scheming little jade, always was."

"Oh no, Humphrey, that is too harsh for words. Beatrice has been very kind, bearing me company in my solitude and diverting me from dismal thoughts and the horrid burden I have had thrust upon me far too soon. I cannot imagine what I would have done without her."

Humphrey raised a disbelieving eyebrow. "Father warned her away, you know, but it would be just like her to come scuttling round as soon as he is in his grave, spinning her webs around you. It *is* her, I can tell by your face. Tell me all about it, and then we shall see what is to be done about it."

Oh, the relief of having a sympathetic ear to listen to all his woes! Dev held nothing back, and Humphrey heard the whole sorry tale, even the kiss, without a single word of condemnation or shock, and, thank God, no hint of disappointment.

"What am I to do, Humph?" Dev said at last. "It is the most dreadful mess, and I cannot see a way out of it."

"Do you want to marry her?" Humphrey said bluntly.

"Good God, no! What do you take me for? I never had the least notion of such a thing."

"You are not entirely lost to what is due to the family, then. All we need to do is to persuade her that it is impossible."

"But how? I have tried already, and none of my arguments weigh with her in the slightest. She is talking about honour and such like, Humph, and is in expectation of an offer. What on earth am I to do?"

"On no account must you offer for her," Humphrey said at once. "Buck up, Dev! Remember that you are a marquess, and no one can make you do anything you do not want to do."

"That is all very well, but even marquesses must not act dishonourably. I *did* kiss her, after all, and it is hardly surprising that she misunderstood, and imagined something more than was intended."

"By all means let us talk about honourable behaviour," Humphrey said, sitting upright and leaning forward. "Let us start with Beatrice herself. What is she doing entering the library alone with you? Why, the door was closed and that was not your doing, I wager! Where is her mama meanwhile? Or any chaperon, come to that. She should not be visiting you unaccompanied, Dev. That is not the behaviour of a respectable young woman. And as for kissing you, and then chasing round after you telling you that you must offer for her — I never heard of anything so forward. Lord, if every young man who kissed a woman had to marry her, then Miss Watson would be arranging her nuptials to a duke's son at this very moment."

Dev laughed at that. "Of course, the notion is idiotic, is it not? And she *was* very forward. She said we were such old friends that it did not matter, but she should not have been here alone, should she? I quite see that now." But then gloom reasserted itself. "Beatrice cannot seriously imagine... But how the devil am I to get rid of her?"

"You could leave here for a while until the fuss dies down."

"Where could I go? I am not supposed to go to London while I am in mourning. Far too rackety, according to Penicuik."

Humphrey rolled his eyes. "He is such an old woman sometimes, but I suppose he has a point. One of the hunting lodges?"

"I could... but I am supposed to be working through these papers of Papa's. So many documents to read over and sign, you have no idea. And Sharp is still trying to instruct me in the finer points of managing the estate."

"On second thoughts, why should you be driven out of your home, just because Beatrice Mallory has got hold of a wrong idea?" Humphrey said thoughtfully. "Dev, a deucedly clever scheme has just entered my head. Beatrice is not in love with you, is she?"

"I... Lord, Humph, how should I know what goes on in her head?"

"Did she cry when you told her you were not going to marry her?"

"Not at all."

"Not upset? Not even a little flustered?"

"On the contrary, she was far less flustered than I was."

"As I thought, not in love with you. So my plan might just work." He chuckled. "It will be amusing to try, anyway, and if it fails, we can still whisk you away from Drummoor. And in the meantime, I shall be always at your side, so that you can never be alone with her. That will keep you safe from the devious little chit."

~~~~~

Humphrey was as good as his word, never leaving Dev unattended even for a moment. He also gave instructions to Crabbe not to admit Miss Mallory unless her mama or sister were with her. The butler seemed unsurprised by this, nodding sagely. Nor would Humphrey permit his brother to walk into the village.

"Oh, certainly, for I should not like to meet Beatrice accidentally," Dev said.
~~~~~

"No, indeed, you do not want to put yourself in her way at all, or add fuel to these rumours. Let her come here, if she wants to see you, and she must do it properly, with a chaperon."

For two days, Beatrice arrived unaccompanied and was advised that Lord Carrbridge and Lord Humphrey were not at home. On the third day, she brought her mother and sister, and spent half an hour in the drawing room making dull conversation before Humphrey rose smoothly to his feet.

"You will forgive us, I am sure, Mrs Mallory, but Lord Carrbridge has a great many matters awaiting his attention just now."

And the ladies had no option but to make their farewells.

"That went off tolerably well," Dev said, as they enjoyed a restorative brandy afterwards. "Beatrice seemed quite amicable, did you not think? Not angry with me? Do you not agree?"

Humphrey chuckled. "She put a good face on it, I have to give her that much credit. But Mrs Mallory would have stabbed you through the heart if she could."

"Oh. Do you think so?"

"I do. In fact, it would not surprise me if we were to have a visit from her very soon."

He was quite right. Two days later, Mrs Mallory's card was brought to the small parlour that Dev had taken over as his private retreat. It was known as the ship room, because the wall panels were adorned with paintings of ships, and he had loved to look at them when he was a boy. The sea had seemed such an impossible concept to him then, and even now it seemed a great wonder that men should sit inside wooden vessels and surrender themselves to the whim of tides and winds and storms in the hope of reaching some far-distant shore, where even the very plants and animals were different from home.

Since his father's death, the ship room had become a cosy refuge from the grandiose splendour, albeit rather faded, of the rest of Drummoor. Here he could read the endless missives from the lawyers, or pore over maps with Sharp, or escape from the watchful eyes of Mr Penicuik and the aunts. And now, here he sat with Humphrey when Crabbe arrived bearing Mrs Mallory's card.

"Just Mrs Mallory, Crabbe? Not the Miss Mallorys?"

"Just Mrs Mallory, my lord, requesting a private interview with your lordship. Shall I tell her you are not at home, my lord?" he added helpfully.

"Oh, heaven save me from private interviews with mamas! What shall I do, Humph?"

"Bring her in here, Crabbe."

"In here, my lord?"

"That is what I said, Crabbe," Humphrey said, winking at him. "Let her think she is being invited into the inner sanctum. But no tea or anything of that nature, Crabbe. She will not be staying long."

Crabbe's eyes twinkled. "Very good, my lord."

While they waited for Mrs Mallory, Dev paced about restlessly. "She is going to ring a peal over me, I daresay," he said gloomily. "Raising expectations, treating her daughter dishonourably and who knows what else besides."

"Now, do not fuss so," Humphrey said. "You need not say anything to her beyond wishing her a good morning."

"Nothing at all?"

"Well... you may ask after her health, I will allow. Smile, be pleasant, the usual thing, as if you are delighted to see her. But you will ask her what you can do for her, as anyone would, you know, and after that I shall take over. Now, spread those papers out on the desk and sit down. You must look busy."

By the time Mrs Mallory was announced, the brothers were bent over the desk, Dev sitting and Humphrey leaning over his shoulder, apparently absorbed in the papers before them.

"Mrs Mallory, my lords."

"Ah, Mrs Mallory, how delightful," Dev said, rising smoothly to his feet. "How are you this morning?"

"Perturbed, Lord Carrbridge. And perplexed."

This was not in the script and Dev looked helplessly at Humphrey, who stepped smoothly into the breach.

"Indeed? Do explain," Humphrey said.

"It is a matter for Lord Carrbridge's ears alone," she said.

"There are no secrets between brothers," Humphrey responded. "I am party to all Lord Carrbridge's dealings. Is that not so, Dev?"

"Oh, yes. Absolutely."

Her eyes narrowed, glancing from one to the other. "Very well. I learn from my daughter that you have misused her, Lord Carrbridge. She is very upset, as you may well imagine. As any respectable lady would be when her reputation is at stake."

"Naturally, you are concerned," Humphrey said quickly, before Dev could respond to this slur.

"I am, Lord Humphrey. I need not scruple to tell you that I am very distressed for my poor Beatrice. She bears it bravely, of course, for never was there a gentler, less selfish creature, but it preys on her mind."

"And as her mother, you must be acutely aware of her every anxiety," Humphrey said. "Indeed, your great sensibility must be awakened to every hurt in your children, no matter how small. Madam, you have my utmost sympathy, but, if I may give you the tiniest hint, I do not think it would be to Miss Mallory's advantage to press this issue just now. As a lady of discernment such as yourself must be aware, such matters are of the utmost delicacy, and the parties concerned are best advised to arrive at a resolution for themselves. Those of us who have their welfare at heart must resist the temptation to interfere, lest we destroy the very thing we seek to nurture. Would you not say so?"

"Oh! Oh yes, my lord, certainly. Not for the world would I interfere."

"Then we must allow nature to take its course, must we not?"

"Indeed, you are quite right. My discernment certainly tells me *that*. It is only my very great fear for my daughter's happiness that prompts this visit, my lord."

"Your feelings do you the utmost credit, madam. I hope your fear has been allayed to some degree and you may now rest easy in the knowledge that time is only wanting to resolve every slight difficulty that stands between the two people concerned."

"You have been most kind, my lord." She simpered, and bobbed him a curtsey.

Humphrey bowed, a little deeper than protocol decreed. "Allow me to escort you to the front door, Mrs Mallory."

"Thank you, my lord. Good day to you, Lord Carrbridge."

Dev stumbled through the usual farewells, and as soon as Humphrey returned, fell on his brother with anguish. "What have you done, Humph? You were supposed to *help* me!"

"Tell me what you thought I said to her," Humphrey said, casting himself into a wing chair.

"You as good as told her that I would marry Beatrice, in time!"

"That is what I wanted her to think, certainly. But what I *actually* said is that they should not push the matter, that you will decide for yourself what you want and that it will all be resolved in time."

"But I—" Dev stopped, confused. "Did you? Oh — I believe you did! Good Lord, that is clever, Humph. I wish I had your brains. It must be very pleasant to be able to come up with these ideas at a moment's notice. My clever schemes take a great deal of thinking about on my part, and even then I am rarely confident in their likely success."

"Frankly, you would get on better if you were to stop thinking altogether, Dev. Your clever schemes usually go badly wrong. Leave the thinking to me."

"I shall certainly do so. Thinking does not agree with me in the least. Even now, I do not quite understand what you did to Mrs Mallory."

"People hear what they want to hear, especially if one speaks with conviction," Humphrey said. "I have been doing a little acting lately, as Henry V no less, so I know all about speaking with conviction. You see, because I told her to step back and allow you and Beatrice the time to work it out for yourselves, she assumed that it will end in an engagement. But I said no such thing, of course. I hope that will give us some respite until my cunning plan comes to fruition."

"Are you going to tell me what it is?"

Humphrey laughed. "No. But you will find out soon enough. Lord, this is fun! I thought being rusticated would be deadly dull but this is almost as entertaining as the Miss Watson affair. How glad I am that I came home!"

"So am I," Dev said fervently. "So am I, Humph."

~~~~~
~~~~~

Two days later a post chaise rolled up the long drive and came to a halt outside the imposing entrance to Drummoor. Crabbe and three footmen descended the steps to attend to the arrivals, but before they could reach the chaise the door was flung open and three young men tumbled out, laughing uproariously. They were still laughing when they were shown into the ship room.

"Well, this is a fine old pile you have here, Humper," said one, a tall, fair young man of about sixteen.

"Humper?" Dev said, trying not to laugh. "You must be a school friend of Humphrey's."

"Rather! Best of friends, so long as I avoid his boxing challenges."

Humphrey grinned. "Dev, may I present to you the Marquess of Ramsey, the Duke of Camberley's eldest. And Robert Stoner of Grantham. And this is... someone I've never seen before in my life," he said, laughing, indicating the third man, somewhat older than the other two.

"My older brother, Andrew," Stoner said. "Here to keep my nose to the grindstone while I'm rusticating. But no need to worry, he won't interfere with your scheme."

"Good," Humphrey said. "The more the merrier. And this is the Earl of— No, damnation, the Marquess of Carrbridge. Keep forgetting."

"You are all very welcome, gentlemen," Dev said. "Am I to take it that this is your mysterious clever plan, Humph?"

"Correct! We have here the heir to a dukedom and the son of one of the richest men in the kingdom, for Stoner's father is a nabob, you know, made a fortune in India. They are going to court Beatrice to entice her away from you, and then we shall see if she wants a title or money, or if it really is you she wants, Dev."

6: A Dinner At Drummoor

With four more young men in the house, all Dev's loneliness vanished. He could see now that the heavy duties of his inheritance, combined with the lack of congenial company, had driven him towards Beatrice in a way that could not have occurred in other circumstances. She was by no means a suitable companion for a man in his position, and he was astonished now that he had ever thought her so. It was one thing to play together as children, but she was a young lady now, looking for a husband, and he was a marquess with a duty to his family to marry well. It was fortunate that Humphrey had arrived to point out the dangers of the situation.

Still, he could not see that Humphrey's plan would succeed.

"Your friends must be very attractive prospects for any young lady," he said, "but they are so young, Humph, younger than Beatrice. She will not look at them."

They were walking down to the lower lake, too energetic to stay cooped up in the house. Ramsey and the two Stoner brothers strode ahead, while Dev and Humphrey lagged behind.

"She will not regard it, I am sure. She knows you are not a certain thing, so she will shift her allegiance if she sees a better opportunity. And if we cannot persuade her to do that, the fellows will chase after the sister instead, so that Beatrice becomes jealous. It will be fine, Dev. You worry too much."

"But she regards herself as betrothed," he said despairingly.

"No such thing! She is trying to take advantage of your good nature by convincing you that there is an obligation, but it is not so. You have made her no promises or spoken of love, or anything of the sort."

"That kiss..." Dev said.

"Which she initiated," Humphrey said sternly. "Good Lord, Dev, what has got into you? You were never used to be so weak-minded. I suppose it comes from being shut up in this place for months, and with only Penicuik and the aunts for company."

"And Sharp. I never knew such a man for talking for hours and saying nothing. He quite wears me out. And the lawyers, Humph! Every day, another letter or a package of documents to sign. It is more than I can bear."

Humphrey looked at him sympathetically. "It must be dreary work, and Father made it look so easy. He should have involved you in that side of things before now."

"Daresay he thought he had time. We all thought he had time. That was what he said about all of you just before he died, that he should have got round to sorting out careers for you sooner."

Humphrey stopped dead. "That makes no sense at all. He was the one who insisted we should *not* think about careers, not for years yet. Told us to enjoy ourselves, and for my part, I intend to follow his advice with great enthusiasm. You must have misheard him, Dev."

"Possibly, although it seemed quite clear at the time. But it *was* odd. He talked about *'all my sons'* because you were all important, as if otherwise one might forget one or two of you. *'Sons of a marquess, ought to be somebody'*, that was what he said, and then he told me to make sure you all had careers so that you could live well."

"Well now, how interesting," Humphrey said. "You must try to remember it exactly, Dev, every word. It might be significant one day. Oh, Lord, Stoner is going to fall in the lake if he goes round that way. Come on, we should warn him off before— Oh, too late, there he goes. Better run and fish him out."

~~~~~

The campaign to woo Miss Mallory began in earnest the following day, when Dev and Humphrey took their visitors down to Lake Cottage to be introduced. A half hour of conversation covered the usual subjects of the weather, the state of the roads and the prospects for the next hunt in exhaustive detail, but it also brought intelligence of a public ball at the nearby town of Sagborough.
~~~~~

A walk around the village afterwards brought several more introductions, and Dev guessed that they would soon be inundated with morning callers wanting a closer look at such interesting young men.

"What a pity we cannot go to this assembly at Sagborough," Dev said, as they walked the short distance home from the village. "I should dearly love a dance. It would be just the thing to cheer me up, I am persuaded. It will be the greatest relief when we can go about more."

"It is certainly too soon for us to be dancing," Humphrey said. "Ramsey and Stoner must go, however, for Beatrice will be there. It is too good an opportunity to waste."

And so they went, but they came back rather downhearted. Beatrice was perfectly affable, they said, but she showed no great interest in either of them.

"It was quite mortifying, actually," said Ramsey, leaning against the mantelpiece in the ship room the next morning. "I am not used to young ladies displaying such indifference towards me. I shall be a duke one day, so if I take an interest in them, they might have the courtesy to show that they appreciate my condescension."

"She wasn't drawn in by my approaches, either," Stoner said. "I made sure to hint regarding Papa's fortune, and my eventual share of it, but I could not gain her attention. Almost she seemed bored," he said indignantly. "Bored! I have never seen such a lack of response in a lady when I mention money. It seemed to me that she was more interested in Andrew."

The elder Mr Stoner shrugged. "I rather liked her, and I suspect ladies respond better when there is genuine interest rather than mere politeness. I am more of an age with her, too. Should you like me to pursue the acquaintance?"

"If it would not inconvenience you too greatly," Humphrey said. "There is no need to marry the girl, after all, just to draw her away from Dev. It might be an amusing diversion for you."

"It would be my pleasure to be of service," he said. "I have nothing else to do while I am here, after all. Papa sent me to keep an eye on Robert and make sure he keeps up with his Greek and so forth while he is rusticated, but that would be a dreadful bore for both of us. I am sure you will forgive me saying so, brother, but the prospect of female company is a vast deal more appealing."

"You will hear no objection from me on that score," his younger brother said. "By all means woo Miss Mallory. Carrbridge, do you plan to hunt at all this season?"

The conversation turned, and no more was said about Beatrice, but Dev could not be easy about it, all the same. When once a lady has declared that she is expecting an offer, he had a suspicion that a gentleman was obliged to make that offer, whether he wished it or not. If only he had not kissed Beatrice! How foolish he had been, even to receive her alone. He was trapped, and when he thought of the prospect of spending the rest of his life with Beatrice smirking at him over the breakfast table, misery overwhelmed him.

~~~~~

There were few advantages to having one's own chapel and chaplain, but one of them was that there was no need to go into the village on a Sunday to attend church. If one chose,
~~~~~

one might go for weeks on end without visiting the village at all. The village, naturally, felt no such restraint and so, apart from the respite afforded by the sabbath, every day brought its share of callers to Drummoor eager to know more of the interesting visitors. The Duke of Camberley was a famous figure in the county, much spoken of but known to few, and the chance to observe his heir at close quarters was too good to miss. The Stoner brothers were less well known, but after their appearance at the assembly, everyone knew their father's income to the nearest hundred pounds and many a young lady now felt a warm interest in their welfare, and an urge to form a better acquaintance with them. Dev and Humphrey were not excluded from attention either, and altogether the prospect of five eligible young men, and not a parent in sight to temper ambition, was all too attractive a draw.

"Are we not to have a moment's peace?" Dev said testily to Humphrey when they were summoned once again to receive callers. "The doorbell has been ringing so much I cannot think straight, and the drawing room is constantly full of women ogling your friends. There is barely time to get dressed in a morning before they start arriving. At any moment I shall have the lawyers posting up here to find out why I have not signed the last set of papers they sent. Is it my fault I have not a minute to myself? No doubt they will then bill me for all the horses and postilions they hired, and the beef and claret consumed on the journey. I should have gone to London."

"Where you would be put to the expense of opening up Marford House," Humphrey said, laughing. "Cheer up! The lawyers must wait on your convenience now. You are a marquess, no one can harry you. But these callers want to see Ramsey and the Stoners. You and me too, of course, but principally the others. So why not give them the opportunity? We have enjoyed a dinner with any number of families lately, so let us hold one of our own."

Dev brightened at once. "Oh yes! What a splendid idea. I have never been so moped in my life, but a dinner — a proper dinner for thirty or forty — would be just the thing. What an excellent fellow you are, Humphrey!"

The dinner galvanised Dev into a frenzy of planning. Given the size of the great hall, he decided that there would need to be sixty covers at least. He and Humphrey compiled a list of every family within twenty miles with whom they dined.

"That is rather a lot of names," Humphrey said dubiously. "Must we write formally to everyone on the list? I have never done such a thing before."

"Mama used to take care of it," Dev said. They were at the breakfast table, and his eye fell on the chaplain. "I say, Penicuik, here is a small task for you. Write the invitations to these people, will you?"

"All of these, my lord? There are more than eighty names on this list, perhaps more than ninety. Are you sure you wish to invite so many? It is a little excessive for a family still in mourning, would you not say? Fifteen or twenty, perhaps — a quiet evening with a little whist, but ninety?"

"They will not all come, I daresay," Dev said airily. "You will not mind helping to write these, for you are so good with the exact titles. I get so muddled about honourables."

"Honourables, my lord?"

"Yes — when someone is called *'The Honourable So-and-so'* and when not. It is all dreadfully confusing. You will oblige me, Penicuik, I am sure, like the good fellow you are."

"Of course, my lord."

A spell of good weather enabled the young men to ride out into the countryside and do a little shooting, and thereby escape the deluge of callers. For the first time since his father's death, Dev began to feel comfortable about his new role. The lawyers could wait, the ladies could wait, everyone could wait, for a man needed to enjoy himself from time to time and not be tied down by the petty details of life. He was a marquess and could give his orders, and his servants would bustle about and fulfil his every whim. He wanted to hold a dinner, and a dinner would be held, but his chef and cook would arrange the menu, the butler would arrange the wine and best china, the housekeeper would ensure every surface gleamed and fires blazed, and Mr Penicuik, bless him, would industriously scribe invitation after invitation, each one correctly addressed. All Dev had to do was to turn up at the appointed hour and enjoy himself.

It was fortunate that the great hall at Drummoor was a large room, and the dining table capable of many extensions, for every single person accepted the invitation, with the exception of one family in deep mourning and Lady Frimble's mother, who had moved into an apartment in her son-in-law's house shortly after the wedding, and had not left it since. Even so, she expected to be invited everywhere, and would send a rudely-worded note to any host or hostess who dared to omit her name from the guest list.

"Ninety-two!" Dev said, appalled when Mr Penicuik informed him of the number of acceptances. "Good God! It is not even a ball or anything in the least fancy. Just a dinner."

Mr Penicuik gave a strained smile. "It is the first formal dinner at Drummoor since — oh, since Lady Carrbridge's health began to decline."

"We have had dinners here, I am certain of it, a great many dinners," Humphrey said, frowning. "We have had the great hall full many times, as I recall."

"Indeed we have, but it was all family," Mr Penicuik said. "Christmas or Easter or a shooting party. Or the late Lord Carrbridge's gentleman friends. Nothing for the county. Everyone is thrilled that you are beginning to entertain in some style, my lord."

"Oh. Well, I rather like the idea, too," Dev said. "Once we are well out of mourning, we shall hold all manner of entertainments, or balls, perhaps, who knows."

"Yes, my lord," Mr Penicuik said tiredly. "Perhaps my lord might wish to engage a secretary for the purpose?"

"Maybe I shall do just that," Dev said. "Mr Penicuik, I should like to offer you the position of secretary. What do you say to that idea?"

"Would there be a salary attached to the post, my lord?"

"Salary? Well, of course there would be a salary. How much would you like?"

For a moment the chaplain goggled at him. Humphrey laughed. "Dev, you must not ask the fellow to name his own salary, you know. How about a hundred a year, Penicuik?"

"Oh, my lord, how generous!"

"Obviously we offered him too much," Humphrey said. "Hmmm..."

Mr Penicuik assumed such a woebegone expression that Dev shook his head, and patted the fellow on the arm. "Take no notice of him, Penicuik. A hundred it shall be, and I daresay you will live very comfortably on that, when it is added to your salary as chaplain."

"The late Lord Carrbridge chose not to pay me a salary for my duties as chaplain, my lord. He always said I could make a handsome sum from the offerings."

"Well, I never put more than sixpence on the offering plate," Dev said indignantly. "I daresay you never made more than a crown or two a week from it. I shall pay an additional salary of one hundred pounds to you as chaplain, Penicuik. There now, you will do very well on two hundred a year, do you not agree?"

But Mr Penicuik was too astonished to say a word.

~~~~~

There was nothing like company for jolting a fellow out of his megrims. The sight of the great hall aglow with candlelight, all the plate and china gleaming, warmed his heart. And when the guests began to arrive, the gentlemen in their finest coats and knee breeches, the ladies in silks and feathers and sparkling jewels, with the hum of lively conversation all around, Dev felt he had finally arrived at his proper place in the world. The deferential bows and curtsies, the respectful murmurs of *'Good evening, Lord Carrbridge. How delightful*
~~~~~

this is, Lord Carrbridge. What a splendid spectacle, Lord Carrbridge,' all served to underscore his position. He was the Earl of Deveron no longer, for he could hold his head high as the Marquess of Carrbridge.

The dinner passed off in the usual manner of such occasions. The roast swan and suckling pig were greatly praised, the spun-sugar replica of Drummoor created gratifyingly loud gasps of admiration and the wine passed around often enough that no one noticed any deficiency in the meal. Lady Frimble led the ladies away to the saloon, the gentlemen enjoyed their port and, all in all, Dev was in a very mellow frame of mind when he made his way through to the saloon to re-join the ladies.

The saloon was crowded, so he took his tea to a quieter part of the room, the better to observe the guests enjoying themselves. To his dismay, he saw Beatrice making her way towards him in determined manner. To this point, he had not exchanged more than half a dozen words with her during the evening, and had not spoken to her at all for a fortnight before that. He had a sinking feeling that the deficiency was about to be made good in no uncertain terms.

"Dev!" she said, and there was something about her smile that chilled him to the bone. "How delightful this is, Dev. I am enjoying the evening immensely."

"Good," he said, but with a nervous tone. "That is very good. Excellent."

"It is very pleasant to see Drummoor used as it should be. I am very happy with everything I have seen. There are only a few changes I shall propose for the future. I did not think there were quite sufficient footmen to serve, leading to some small delays, but that is easily rectified. The main problem I saw was with the ill-matched china. Two different styles in use at once — I never saw anything so embarrassing! I shall want a properly matched set for the future."

"That is a family tradition," Dev said. "When the third marquess married, his two aunts each gave a dinner service to the bridal pair. To avoid offending either of them, both sets are used for grand dinners. That is how it has been done for more than a hundred years now."

She laughed, but he thought she coloured slightly, perhaps embarrassed at not knowing this piece of Marford family history. "Even so, it looks so odd, do you not agree? We need not be bound by the actions of our long-dead ancestors. I do not imagine they care much whether the china matches or not."

"No, but I do," Dev said. "I like the family tradition. It amuses me, and therefore I shall continue to use both sets of china."

For a moment she looked discomfited, but she rallied swiftly. "As you please, of course. It shall be ever my desire to ensure your happiness."

This was an odd thing to say, and Dev could find no response, but she needed none. "As to the food, I have no fault to find. The cooks are both excellent, and I shall not need to make any changes in the kitchen."

Dev tried to stop his mouth falling open. “Changes?” he said, his voice rather strangled.

“Yes, changes. In the future. When we are married.”

7: A Quarrel

For a moment, the room seemed to be spinning and Dev could not catch his breath. Married? What was she talking about? She smiled up at him, and for a moment he felt the walls closing in around him. But something tugged at him, some sense of urgency. He knew, as if by instinct, that he could not let this pass. If he did, he would be rolled up and the banns would be called before he could turn round.

To give himself time to think, he said, "I have not the pleasure of knowing what you are talking about."

She tittered, and to his ears it was a brittle sound. "Why, Dev, I am talking about the changes I plan to make in the future. When I am the Marchioness of Carrbridge."

Inside him, two impulses warred. On the one hand, one and twenty years of upbringing as a gentleman told him not to contradict a lady, nor to speak harshly to her, lest her delicate sensibilities be overwrought. Ladies were fragile creatures, to be handled like porcelain and addressed with the utmost civility. Even if one were required to correct a lady's behaviour, one must do it with the utmost gentleness, lest — oh, the horror! — she be reduced to tears. But on the other hand, one and twenty years of upbringing as a nobleman told him to depress the pretensions of anyone of lower birth who presumed to be his equal. The sheer effrontery before him raised his ire, and so that night it was the nobleman who won. Dev drew himself up to his full height and gazed down at her disdainfully.

"You forget yourself, Miss Mallory. If ever I should honour you with the title of Marchioness of Carrbridge, I should only do so in the proper form, by first obtaining your mother's consent, by courting you in the accepted manner and finally, by making a clear offer for your hand. None of these have I done, and I think I should have remembered if I had. Nor do I have the least intention of doing so, and if you have deluded yourself into thinking that I should, you have only yourself to blame."

He stopped, his breathing heavy, uncomfortably aware that he was speaking rather louder than he had intended. The silence in the room was profound, as heads swivelled and eyes turned towards him. Beatrice stared at him, ashen-faced, eyes wide with shock. Was she going to cry? He had the most terrible dread of seeing a lady cry, and perhaps if she had done so matters might have gone very differently. But she did not, standing rigid and silent before him.

They stood thus for what seemed an eternity. Even so, Dev jumped when a discreet cough sounded at his elbow. He turned unseeing eyes towards the intruder, and for a moment could not for the life of him remember who the fellow was.

"Forgive me, Lord Carrbridge, but Miss Dunborough has agreed to play for those who wish to dance. Miss Mallory, I should be very honoured if I might claim the first dance with you."

Beatrice looked at him with the same incomprehension that Dev felt, but she recovered herself in an instant. "Why, thank you, Mr Stoner. I should be delighted. Pray excuse me, Lord Carrbridge."

Stoner! The older brother, who had said once before that he liked Beatrice. That was quick-thinking indeed, stepping in to rescue them from the awkward moment. Beatrice made her curtsy to Dev, Stoner bowed and then led her away with every appearance of pleasure. All around the room, conversation resumed and Dev breathed deeply, allowing his rapid heartbeats to slow to a normal level.

"For God's sake, Dev, whatever have you done?" Humphrey hissed at his elbow. "Come through to the tapestry room and have some brandy."

The tapestry room was designed as a masculine retreat from the female domination of the saloon, a place where a man could refresh himself away from his wife's eyes, and talk about politics or the hunt or exploits of a more private nature. A couple of card tables had been set up, and a pair of footmen were on hand to dispense in a liberal manner the best port or brandy.

Humphrey grabbed two glasses and shoved one into Dev's hand. "There! Get that down you... good. And another."

"Are you trying to get me drunk, Humph?" Dev said indignantly. "No intention of getting drunk. Tried it once, it was a miserable business, and I was sick as a dog all the next day." He set the second glass down so sharply on a nearby table that it shattered, spilling blood-red wine onto the carpet. "Not drinking any more."

"As you please, but do calm down."

"Calm down? *Calm down!* Did you hear what she said? *'When I am Marchioness of Carrbridge!'* Unbelievable, quite unbelievable! The presumption of the girl — it is not to be borne, not to be borne!"

Sir Richard Frimble shifted in his seat at the nearest card table to look round at them, the chair creaking under his weight. "Is it Beatrice Mallory you speak of, Carrbridge? Ha! Lady Frimble told me that the girl and that sly mother of hers have been puffing it all around that she has an understanding with you, dear boy. Never saw it myself, not with your father barely cold in his grave and your poor mama so far away."

"Exactly so!" Dev said. "Never had the least thought of it, and so I told her, but will she listen? But I will *not* be bounced into it as if I were a stable boy caught fiddling with the dairymaid and needing to be shamed into doing the honourable thing. I never said a word about marriage to her, never made her an offer, never made love to her, not once. There is *nothing* between us, and never was, and if she thinks she can force me into it, she had better think again."

"Quite right, Carrbridge!" Sir Richard said. "You, a marquess, marry a nobody like Beatrice Mallory? Hardly likely! Do not let yourself be bamboozled by the wiles of women. Beatrice Mallory a marchioness, indeed. Ha! There are some who came tonight in the expectation of an announcement, but not anyone who knows those encroaching Mallory women, I do assure you. Why, we had Beatrice sniffing around Arthur last spring, and he is such a gudgeon he almost fell for her cunning ways, too, the foolish boy. Luckily, I saw her off and he is more satisfactorily settled now, may God be praised."

"Father warned Beatrice away a couple of years ago," Humphrey said.

"Aye, she likes to try her luck," Sir Richard said. "Gave her a set-down, did you, Carrbridge? Good! About time someone did. She thinks far too well of herself, that girl. She had an offer from a very nice clergyman the first year she was out, but that was not grand enough for her, apparently." He chuckled. "Made a bit of a scene, did you?"

"I rather fear that I did," Dev said ruefully. "No idea what I said, for I was too angry to mind my tongue. I daresay I shall have to apologise to her. Was I very bad, Humph?"

"Pretty bad, although… it was all true, every word. But still, it would have been better not to speak so loud that everyone in the room could hear."

Sir Richard laughed so hard he dropped his cards. "Great heavens, Carrbridge, you are turning into a wonderful asset for the county. First you decide to entertain in a style not seen at Drummoor for years, for which office we are all very much obliged to you, you may be sure, and then you have a set-to with a young lady in the middle of your own dinner party. You have admirable spirit, young man, quite admirable." And, still chortling, he set the chair creaking again as he turned back to his game.

"Did she really say she was going to be the Marchioness of Carrbridge?" Humphrey said in a low tone, pushing another glass into Dev's hand and leading him to a quiet corner.

"She did. Said there were not enough footmen and she disliked the two sorts of china."

"But that is part of our history! Good Lord, did she think we could not afford a matching set of plates, like some upstart provincial?"

Dev snorted with laughter. "Oh, but she approved of the cooking. She will not make any changes in the kitchen, she informs me. Is that true — that Father warned her away? Oh, but I remember Hatty saying something of the sort — some fuss that blew up while I was away at Aunt Juliana's. Never knew quite what it was about. And then we never saw the Mallorys again until after Father died. It does seem—" He broke off, mesmerised by the glass in his hand. "Lord, Humph, what is this you have given me? You promised me brandy. Timothy, some brandy here. And take this stuff away. Ah, that is much better!" He drank deeply, and sighed with pleasure. "I begin to feel more like myself. But tell me the truth, Humphrey, am I in trouble with this Beatrice business? I shall not have to marry the hussy, shall I?"

"I will confess, I was afraid that might be the way of it," Humphrey said. "It is not good form to humiliate a girl like that, even if she *was* asking for it. But as Sir Richard sees no obligation, I am a little easier about it. Even so… I wish Mama were here!" he said abruptly. "This is a devilish confusing business, and I should like Mama's opinion on the matter. She always knows what is to be done."

"Or Father," Dev said thoughtfully. "I had not realised until now just how much I depended on him to... well, to protect me from this sort of thing. Whenever I went into society, he was always there, keeping an eye on me, steering me away from trouble. *'Not that one,'* he would say, *'she may be pretty as paint, but her father is a vulgar mushroom.'* Or, *'That one will be nothing but trouble.'* I used to think him overbearing, but he was looking after me, I can see that now. And as soon as he is gone, I have got myself into a dreadful mess and I am not at all sure how to get out of it. But one thing is certain — I shall not, under any circumstances, marry Beatrice Mallory, and there is an end to it. If I am ostracised by the *ton*, then so be it."

Humphrey chewed his lip. "Yes, but what if *she* is ostracised by society, Dev? Suppose everyone believes that she has been jilted, and laughs at her? She will have no reputation left. What shall you do then?"

~~~~~

Dev's spirits had never been lower. Even in the dark days of his father's sudden illness and unexpected death, there had been that gleam of optimism — he would be the Marquess of Carrbridge, in full possession of his inheritance, and that was a fine thing at the age of one and twenty. He was not so sure now just how fine it was. It seemed to him that his path was fraught with difficulties. The legal business was tricky, the management of his estates was confusing and even moving in society was perilous, with no one to advise him how to go on. Mr Penicuik was too cautious, but perhaps that would have been better than holding such a large gathering, for all their acquaintance to witness his humiliation of Beatrice.
~~~~~

Beatrice. Whenever he thought of her, he ground his teeth in frustration. He had been foolish to allow himself to be on such easy terms with her, but she had taken advantage of him, he could see that clearly now. All those times she had come alone to the house on some pretext or other — the music room, or the books in the library. Why had he not realised how he was being manipulated? And then she had deliberately fallen against him and kissed him, and he had been too surprised to resist her.

But telling the world that they were as good as engaged, and talking to him openly about the day when she would be the Marchioness of Carrbridge? No, that was *not* acceptable, nor was it the behaviour of a sensible, modest young lady. She was not in any way worthy to be mistress of Drummoor, and he would never allow it, no matter how high a price he had to pay. Even so, he did not want her to be an object of ridicule, to be pointed out as one who was jilted by a marquess, even if she had brought the situation on herself. Yet he had no idea what could be done about it. Thus his thoughts ran constantly, chasing each other round his head like mice in the attic.

Directly after breakfast he had gone to apologise in the most abject terms for his behaviour, and even though Beatrice had accepted his apology composedly and said she was sorry too, for misunderstanding him, he had felt dreadful about the whole affair and wished with all his heart that he had managed it better. It was a sad beginning to his life as a marquess. He was a peer of the realm, and a man of some consequence, yet he had run aground almost before he had set sail.

He was sunk in gloom in the ship room later that morning, ranting to a sympathetic but unhelpful Humphrey, and trying to prepare himself for the onslaught of curious morning callers which would begin at any moment, when there was a knock on the door. It opened immediately to reveal the elder Mr Stoner's face, wreathed in an apologetic expression.

"Beg pardon for disturbing you, Lord Carrbridge. I wonder if I might have a word?"

"Of course, Stoner. Have as many words as you wish, for I am sorely in need of some distraction just now."

"It is about Miss Mallory."

"Beatrice? Is it bad news? Something that will make me even more in the dismals?"

"As to that, I could not say," Stoner said, with a half smile. "I just wished to... that is to say, I wanted to be sure that... you see, the thing is—"

"Spit it out, like a good fellow," Humphrey said. "And no need to look so nervous. We will not bite your head off."

"I should not like to overstep the mark, Lord Carrbridge," Stoner said. "Push you aside, or tread on your toes, or... or anything of that nature."

"Lord, Stoner, you talk in riddles," Dev said crossly. "Speak plain, man."

Humphrey began to laugh. "It is all right, Dev. I believe Stoner brings us good tidings."

Stoner licked his lips, and began to speak in a great rush, his cheeks pink. "Am I correct in thinking that you have no intention of marrying Miss Mallory yourself? Because if that is so, I should very much like to take some steps in that direction myself. Got to know her quite well lately, and... and rather like her, and should very much like—"

Dev let out a great whoop of delight. "You are going to marry Beatrice?"

"Well... if she will have me," Stoner said, with a shy smile. "Not spoken yet, naturally. Had no wish to get in your way, my lord, so I kept out of it. But then you had your *contre-temps* and I saw my opportunity. However, I should not like to take her away from you, if—"

"Take her and welcome," Dev said. "In fact, *please* take her, and the sooner the better, for I have been so plagued with the business, you cannot imagine. Got myself onto very sticky ground, all quite unintentionally. Never meant the least harm, and would never hurt her for the world but as to marrying her — no, quite impossible. It has been a great worry to me, so if you can pull it off, I shall be most deeply obliged to you. But... do you really care for the chit? And will your father accept it? The Mallorys are not exactly high in society, you know, and with his fortune he might have expected you to bring home a duke's daughter."

"I do, I do care for her!" Stoner said eagerly. "I care for her very much. She is exactly the sort of woman I like — practical, sensible, not prone to weeping and wailing. I was so struck by her bravery when you said... well, all those things. She did not *collapse* or have hysterics or make a scene."

"No, I believe she was a great deal more dignified than I was," Dev said sorrowfully. "I made the most tremendous scene, and embarrassed a lady, and one of my oldest friends. It was unforgivable, although she accepted my apology very gracefully. Poor Beatrice! She may have been a little forward, but she deserved better from me than that. If you can win her hand and her heart, Stoner, I shall be very glad indeed to see her happily settled."

"Thank you, my lord! If I am so fortunate as to secure her affection, we shall do very well together, I assure you. And Papa will be very happy. We are not exactly high in society ourselves, and Papa has never expected any of us to marry a noblewoman. He is not in the least ambitious. In fact, he was very concerned about Robert mixing with you and Ramsey, in case he got above himself. No, my father will be very satisfied with my choice."

"Then have at it, Stoner, with my blessing, and may your endeavours meet with every success."

Epilogue

"Ugh! This tea is cold," Lord Carrbridge said.

"You have been so intent on relating your story that you quite forgot it," his wife said. "Let me send for a fresh pot, or should you like a glass of Madeira? Or brandy, perhaps?"

"Madeira, I think." He watched her cross the room to the console and pour from the decanter, admiring the graceful way she moved. "Ah, my angel, how glad I am that I waited until you crossed my path. But now you may appreciate why I was so nervous about showing my feelings for you until I was sure we were quite right for each other. I had the greatest dread of making another dreadful mistake."

"I can see that," she said, sitting down beside him again, and taking his free hand in hers. "Beatrice sounds like a scheming hussy."

"You are inclined to blame her for what happened, then?" he said, brightening. "But no, that is not really fair. She wanted to fix her interests with me, certainly, and she went about it in a particularly forthright way — so typical of Beatrice! But I blame myself, for I should have been more wary. And to humiliate her in public! That was not the way a gentleman should act towards a lady."

"We cannot always be perfectly wise, and do everything exactly as we should," she said gently. "You were sad and lonely and overwhelmed, and she took advantage of you rather, which she should not have done. But then I daresay she was terrified that her younger sister would outshine her, and felt she could not wait — no wonder she was inclined to push you! But her mama should never have allowed her to be so forward, and you cannot be blamed for taking her overtures as mere sympathetic friendship, not when you were in mourning. Perhaps you did not handle the situation as well as you might, but it is my belief that Beatrice was greatly at fault for scheming to entice you. But then I schemed a little, too. Do you remember?"

"Your schemes were enchanting," he said, smiling down at her. "And you never tried to trick me into marrying you, only to put me into a romantic state of mind with poetry and flowers, which is not at all the same."

"And did Mr Stoner marry Beatrice in the end?" she said.

"He did, and they have been very happy. They came to London once or twice when they were first married, and I introduced them into my set, but I am not sure that Beatrice quite liked it, for they have stayed in Grantham for the last few years."

"I daresay she did not like being someone of no great importance to the *ton*, when she could be the centre of attention in a smaller society. Do you know, my love, I think you must have changed a great deal since those days, for by the time you came into Brinshire, you were very comfortable with your position in society."

"Certainly I became used to it, that is true. Mama came home very soon after my trouble with Beatrice, and once I could talk to her, I did very well."

"I should have liked to know your mama," Connie said. "She sounds like a very wise woman."

"She was. I was so happy to see her again, although she was very ill by then, so pale and thin. She liked to have Harriet attend her, but it was three days before she was well enough to see me..."

~~~~~

"Here he is now, Mama," Harriet said. "Have a comfortable coze, you two, but not for too long, understand?" She crept out of the room, shutting the door behind her with a soft click.

"Ah, Francis! Come closer. There is a chair by the bed for you."

She was propped up on the pillows, her face almost as white as the linen, her breathing laboured. He sat, and took her bony fingers in his, and kissed them.

"I am so glad to see you again, Mama, you cannot imagine."

"You have been having an interesting time of it, I hear, but it all came out well in the end."
~~~~~

"Fortunately for me. I was so terrified I should end up married to Beatrice."

"I should never have permitted it," his mother said. "I count Annie as a very dear friend, but she knows perfectly well that her daughters are not suitable brides for Drummoor. Of course, if you had been in love with the girl that would have been different, and I should have made her very welcome. No one should marry without some affection in the case. But when there is none, and, even worse, when there is trickery involved — no, that would be wrong. But you will be plagued by ambitious women, I am afraid. Your father kept them at bay when he was alive, but now you will have to learn to deal with them yourself. They will not all be nobodies like Beatrice Mallory, either, to be easily sent packing. If you pay too much attention to a nobleman's daughter and raise expectations, you could easily find yourself under an obligation and society will not readily forgive you if you do not do the honourable thing. So you must be very careful, and make sure that a young lady is exactly right before you show your intentions."

"I will, but it all sounds so difficult, and if I get it wrong, I will have to marry."

"You are a marquess, Francis, so you never *have* to do anything you do not wish to. And you are a man. Society is far more forgiving of male lapses in judgement. Even so, it would be very uncomfortable to defy the proprieties and you do not like to be made uncomfortable, I think. Some of your brothers would not regard it, but you would find it distressing to be ostracised, even in a slight way. You do well in male company, your father always said, but you are as yet unsure of yourself with ladies, so that is where you must take the greatest care. You need someone to look after you, as your father did."

"Humphrey has been very good since he has been here."

"He is still young, however, and although his judgement is good, he has not yet any great experience of the world. I shall invite my brother Lucius for a visit, I believe."

"Oh, I like Uncle Lucius!"

"Good. He is one of those bachelors who knows everyone and is invited everywhere, for his manners are impeccable. Very good *ton,* is Lucius. Get to know him well, and make sure you keep him close when you move in society and follow his advice. He will keep you safe."

The door opened again, and Harriet appeared. "Time for Dev to go, Mama. I do not want you getting overtired."

His mother smiled. "They still call you Dev. How funny!"

"I still think of myself as Dev," he said with an answering smile. "I was the Earl of Deveron for a long time, after all. Besides..." He frowned. "It sounds wrong when people call me Lord Carrbridge. That is — was — Father, and I do not feel ready to take his place yet. I am not sure I will ever be ready. He was a great man, and I feel very inadequate by comparison."

"You must not idolise your father," his mother said. "You saw the public side of him — the political orator, the leader of men who moved with the greatest ease through society. But there was another side to him which was less worthy, as I am sure you will discover in time. All men have their weaknesses, as well as their strengths. You have your strengths, too,

Francis, so you must never regard yourself as inferior to anyone. You are the Marquess of Carrbridge, which is an honourable title with a long history, and you will add to the line splendidly. You may hold your head up and stand tall in any company, even the highest in the land, never forget that. It will take you a while to grow into the role, that is all, and if your sister and brothers want to continue to call you Dev for the time being, there is no harm in that. Now I am ready for a nap, so off you go. We will talk again soon."

~~~~~

"And did you discover anything unworthy of your father?" Connie said.

"Only the usual things — gambling, mostly. He liked to bet on everything and anything. I have heard so many tales of his wagers, with whole estates changing hands on the outcome. Silly things, too, like whether one of his friends could hop for the full length of St James's Street. I believe he won that one. There were women involved, too."

"You mean betting on who would be the first to kiss her? Or bed her? Marry her, perhaps?"

"No, nothing like that. I have no idea what they were betting on, but one of them — an earl, I believe — was short of funds to lay down, and no one would take his vowels, so he staked his daughter on the outcome."

"You mean, if he lost the bet he would have to hand over his daughter?" Connie said, hands to mouth in amazement. "How deliciously rackety. But how horrible for the lady herself. And did he lose? Did he really gamble away his daughter?"
~~~~~

"No one seems to remember that part of the story."

"Oh, how typical of men, to remember the bet but not what became of the lady involved," she said indignantly.

"You are quite right," Lord Carrbridge said. "I shall ask around, and see if I cannot find out how it all ended. Perhaps the earl won the bet and the lady was spared such humiliation. Ah, Crabbe, what is it?"

The butler sidled hesitantly into the room, not quite comfortable about entering her ladyship's sitting room, which were feminine quarters, and therefore not a place for any self-respecting butler to venture. But his lordship was often there, and thus he was required to gird his loins and enter therein.

"The mail, my lord, my lady."

He held out a silver salver, with letters neatly divided into two piles, one larger than the other.

"Thank you, Crabbe," the marquess said, as the butler withdrew as hastily as his dignity permitted. "Only two for you today, my love."

"And this one is only from my milliner, so that can wait. Oh, this is from Cousin Mary."

"Lady Hardy? How is poor Sir Osborne? Is there any improvement?"

"None at all, in fact he is worse, and fading fast, Mary says. He will not see Christmas, she fears."

"Ah, the poor man! No more than a month left on earth. But at least his suffering will soon be over. Poor Mama lingered on for years, slowly declining day by day and month by month. Consumption is a terrible affliction, Connie, and I would not wish it on my greatest enemy."

"No, indeed."

"How is Lady Hardy bearing it? It was not a love match, but they hold each other in some affection, I believe."

"Very much so. I thought it an odd pairing at first, but they have been very happy for the brief time they have been together. Not even four years. It is very sad." She sighed, and turned back to her letter. "Mary was ever practical, so she does not give way to grief, but she must feel it most acutely. It is typical of her that her thoughts are not for herself but for Sir Osborne, and his cousin who will now inherit."

"Her position will be awkward," Lord Carrbridge said. "Sir Osborne's mother still lives in the house, does she not?"

"Yes, and has the heir and his wife very much under her thumb. But Mary is most concerned about Mr Merton's position."

"Merton? Sir Osborne's friend?"

"Friend and secretary, but the new baronet will not need a secretary, and Sir Osborne's mother has always had a dislike of Mr Merton. Mary is very much afraid that she will send him packing as soon as Sir Osborne has breathed his last."

"Poor fellow. But he will find a new position, I daresay."

"In time, certainly, but— Oh, Francis, I have had an idea."

He brightened. "Excellent! You always have the most splendid ideas, my angel."

"You have fretted for years over Mr Sharp's management of your money, and always having to ask for funds and never knowing quite where it comes from. Why not engage Mr Merton to look into things and advise you on the value of your estates? Perhaps he could arrange matters so that you do not always have to go through Mr Sharp when you need money? Mr Sharp is a very good sort of land agent, I believe, but I do not at all see why he has control of your money."

"By Jupiter, I think you may have hit on something! Merton is a straight sort of fellow, for all he looks so dismal all the time, and he would give me honest answers about my affairs. I shall write at once. Oh, but how awkward. What shall I say? *'Do come as soon as Sir Osborne is dead'* is a little... unfortunately worded. Might you help me to compose something, my love? You are so good at letter-writing, for you are always writing to all your relations. And mine, come to that."

"Of course. Come, sit at your escritoire, and I shall think up a clever way to invite Mr Merton here."

"Thank you, my love. I am very glad I have you to help me with such tasks."

"You really should have a secretary, a man in your position."

"I had one for a few weeks, until the tragic accident. Poor Mr Penicuik."

"The chaplain? What happened to him?"

"We never speak of it, for it was far too dreadful. I am ready. *'Dear Merton,'* What shall I say next?"

She hesitated. "I take it you do not mind him poking around in your affairs? I mean, who knows what he may find out about your family?"

"I doubt we have any secrets to be discovered. A peer of the realm is a public figure, whose life is lived in full view of anyone interested. It is like being a performer on a stage — everyone sees everything we do."

"All families have secrets," she said. "Look at mine if you want proof of how even the most respectable family may have mysteries in its history."

"I doubt there is anything yet to be discovered in mine, but if there is, Merton is welcome to uncover it. *'Dear Merton, I am writing to you to...'* Now what shall I write?"

She pulled her chair nearer to his and began to dictate.

THE END

If you'd like to find out just what Mr Merton discovers about the late marquess and the family fortune, look out for the rest of the series *Sons of the Marquess.* Book 1 is *Lord Reginald*, and you can read a sneak preview of Chapter 1 after the acknowledgements.

The story of how the Marquess of Carrbridge met Miss Connie Allamont and, after many misunderstandings, married her is told in *Connie: The Daughters of Allamont Hall Book 3*, part of a series about the six Allamont sisters whose father leaves them large dowries in his will, but only on condition that they marry in order of age.

You can find details of these and all my books on my website http://marykingswood.co.uk.

Thanks for reading!

I hope you enjoyed reading this novella, which is free as a thank you for signing up to my mailing list. You'll also hear about new releases, special deals and occasional giveaways and competitions, but you can unsubscribe at any time.

A note on historical accuracy: I have endeavoured to stay true to the spirit of Regency times, and have avoided taking too many liberties or imposing modern sensibilities on my characters. The book is not one of historical record, but I've tried to make it reasonably accurate. However, I'm not perfect! If you spot a historical error, I'd very much appreciate knowing about it so that I can correct it and learn from it. Thank you!

About the series Sons of the Marquess: *the Ninth Marquess of Carrbridge is happily married to the former Miss Constance Allamont, he has an heir and a spare in the nursery, and all seems set fair for a life of perfect bliss. His five younger brothers are a bit of a handful, but young men like to spread* *their wings a bit. If only they weren't so expensive! And whatever happened to that huge income his father used to boast about? It seems to have vanished in a generation. And now there's the unknown son of his father's who claims to be the legitimate heir. It's a bit much for a Marquess to deal with. Fortunately, his wife has some ideas about restoring their fortunes...*

Book 0: The Earl of Deveron (a prequel novella, free to mailing list subscribers)

Book 1: Lord Reginald

Book 2: Lord Humphrey

Book 3: Lord Augustus

Book 4: Lord Montague

Book 5: Lord Gilbert

Any questions or comments about the series? Email me at mary@marykingswood.co.uk- I'd love to hear from you!

About the author

I write traditional Regency romances under the pen name Mary Kingswood, and epic fantasy as Pauline M Ross. I live in the beautiful Highlands of Scotland with my husband. I like chocolate, whisky, my Kindle, massed pipe bands, long leisurely lunches, chocolate, going places in my campervan, eating pizza in Italy, summer nights that never get dark, wood fires in winter, chocolate, the view from the study window looking out over the Moray Firth and the Black Isle to the mountains beyond. And chocolate. I dislike driving on motorways, cooking, shopping, hospitals.

Acknowledgements

Thanks go to:

Shayne Rutherford of Darkmoon Graphics for the cover

My beta readers: Clara Benson, Mary Burnett

Last, but definitely not least, my first reader: Amy Ross.

Sneak preview: Lord Reginald: Chapter 1

Lord Reginald Marford was uncommonly nervous. The summons itself was out of the ordinary, but the serious demeanour of his oldest brother about the matter was enough to concern any man. The Marquess of Carrbridge was, as a rule, the most easy-going and affable of brothers, never letting any setback disturb his equanimity. If some extraordinary event should manage to ruffle his feathers, then the marchioness was sure to smooth everything out in the most delightful manner. Nothing was permitted to interfere with the regular round of pleasure which any well-born family expected to pursue. In such comfortable ways, life had gone on in the Marford family for generations.

But now, it appeared, all was gloom, the marquess was miserable and even his wife's good humour was replaced by anxious fluttering and an unusually short temper. It was not right that such a charming lady should have even the smallest worry to distract her, when her beauty and accomplishments entitled her to a life of unalloyed happiness. Such were Lord Reginald's thoughts as he made his way down the oak-panelled staircase at Drummoor to the great hall.

Monty was there first, naturally. No matter how punctual one might be, Monty was always there first.

"Is it going to be bad, Reggie?" he said at once, raising those huge, innocent eyes to his older brother. Reggie was only six years older than Monty, but sometimes he felt very old, far older than his nine and twenty years.

"I think it might be," Reggie said.

"It is all my fault, I know it," Monty said, twisting his hands together. "I should never have bought that pair from Longman. I was completely taken in, for he told me they were such fine animals, and they certainly looked it. Such a bargain, as I thought at the time, but it was not so. I am sure we will have to retrench and it is all my fault."

"Nonsense, Monty, but you should remember to take Gus with you next time. He knows everything there is to know about horseflesh."

"Oh, I tried to! I told Longman I would wait until Gus was back from Devon, but he would not have it. He had another buyer, you see, and the deal could not wait even another day, so what could I do but close with him at once?"

"You could have called his bluff. He bamboozled you, and that is the size of it. But you need not despair, for your doings have been nothing to Gil's, and even Humphrey has been losing at the tables lately. If we are in the basket, it will not be because of that broken-winded pair Tom Longman managed to foist on you."

Monty tried a smile, managed only a lop-sided quirk of the lips and abandoned the attempt. "But it is going to be bad, I feel sure."

"Everything that Merton fellow has a hand in is bad, it seems to me," Reggie said gloomily. "He has a face like a wet Sunday in Lincoln. There is no joy in him, and he delights in making everyone else's lives as joyless as his own."

"Oh no, Reggie, I am sure you are mistaken," Monty said. "He is a very good sort of man, I think."

Reggie sighed. "I am out of sorts today and not minded to be fair, but nevertheless I cannot dispute the point with you. He is indeed a most worthy sort of person, and was there ever anything more dispiriting than such a man?"

Monty managed a genuine smile. "You are just cross because he defeated you at chess."

Chess was the least of his worries, but Reggie managed a smile. "A perfectly valid reason to be cross with anyone, I should think. I would not mind so much if he would be so obliging as to lose occasionally. Not every time, for I am not unreasonable, but once a week or so would be enough to make me happy. Is it asking so much? It would be a politeness in him as a guest, considering that he eats our partridge and drinks our claret, and never even looks as if he enjoys it. Ah, here are Humphrey and Gus."

The third and fourth Marford brothers were laughing at some private joke, but seeing the long faces on Reggie and Monty, Humphrey said, "Cheer up, you two! How bad can it be, truly? If we are really under the hatches, we must all marry heiresses to set ourselves straight. Ladies love a lord, you know."

"They love a peer," Reggie said, determined not to cheer up. "Being the mere brother of a marquess is less appealing."

"Nonsense!" Humphrey said. "They all want to be Lady Something-or-other. But if matrimony holds no attraction for you, Reggie, you might think about taking up a career."

Reggie shuddered. "Lord, no! Can you see me in the army, galloping about with a sword in my hand? Far too energetic for me. And as for the church, that is not energetic enough. No, I should infinitely sooner find myself an heiress."

"Heiresses are always bracket-faced," Gus said. "I prefer my horses, thank you all the same."

"Ah, but will we have any horses left us after Merton has done his work?" Monty said.

Gus's expression turned instantly to alarm. "No! Carrbridge would not — would he?"

"We must all make sacrifices," Humphrey said, his smile suggesting that he had no serious fears of such a thing. "One hunter instead of two or three, perhaps, and you might have to give up one of your curricles, Gus."

"It is all very well for you," Gus said. "You do well enough at cards to keep you in style, but I seem to have done nothing but lose lately."

"You will not attend to the play," Humphrey said. "You get distracted too easily."

"Ah, here is Hattie," Reggie put in quickly, before the two could lapse into their familiar debate. "And Carrbridge and Connie. Excellent."

The marquess and marchioness made a handsome couple, but their usual smiles were absent today. Lady Harriet Marford, by contrast, wore an expression of determined cheerfulness.

"What a delightful family gathering," she asked. "Why so Friday-faced, everyone? No one has died, you know. Are we all here?"

"Still awaiting Gil," Reggie said.

"Perhaps we should wait," the marquess said, looking about the hall anxiously, as if he expected the youngest Marford brother to be lurking behind a pillar or hiding in the suit of armour at the foot of the stairs, ready to pop out at any moment to surprise them.

"Who knows when he might appear?" the marchioness said briskly. "Best get this over with, do you not agree, Lord Carrbridge?"

"Yes, indeed, my love. Let us go in."

The library at Drummoor was as large as a ballroom, and was indeed used for that purpose once or twice each winter when its three massive fireplaces almost kept the room warm enough for comfort. Now, in January, it was as cold as an ice house, and almost as cheerless, the endless shelves of books filling every wall and the dark-painted ceiling giving it the appearance of a cave. Reggie would not be surprised to spy bats hanging from the chandeliers. As a boy, he had always been terrified of the place, scene of the weekly summoning by his grandfather to be shown a new treasure — a stuffed peacock, perhaps, or a map of Persia, or a bone knife from some long-lost tribe — followed by a lecture on the ingratitude of the French peasantry, or the colonials, or whoever was in revolt at the time. The seventh marquess was long in his grave, but the familiar dread still settled in Reggie's stomach as he crossed the library floor.

The assembled Marfords filed past long lines of glass-topped display cases housing the collections of former marquesses — eggs, feathers, decorated snuff boxes, pocket watches, strange assortments of bones and numerous sets of miniature chess pieces, enamelled or bejewelled or carved or gilded into a variety of fanciful shapes. At the far end of the room, the vast arched window depicted in stained glass the triumphant ride of the Earl of Deveron to the king's aid in the civil war, which resulted in the grateful monarch immediately raising him to the title of Marquess of Carrbridge.

Beneath the window, and painted in jewel colours by the glass, sat a desk large enough for a score of people to dine in tolerable comfort. Behind it, sombrely attired, Daniel Merton stood awaiting them, bowing. Reggie had no great liking for Merton, for he was sober to a fault, and what could be worse than a man who never gambled or drank to excess or even took a mistress? He was a decent rider, Reggie had to give him credit for that, but there was something unnatural about a man who enjoyed rummaging about with old documents and ledgers. And then there was his irritating skill at chess. No, Reggie could not like him.

Chairs were already arranged in front of the desk, and Merton waited politely while they disposed themselves, Carrbridge and the two ladies in front, the rest behind, and one empty chair for Gil. Only then did Merton bow again and take his seat, and even his air of deference irritated Reggie that day.

"My lord?" Merton said politely.

"Yes, yes, do begin. We will not wait for Gil."

"As your lordship wishes. I have completed my initial assessment of the state of your estate, my lord. It has not been as complete or as detailed an investigation as I should have liked, for not all the relevant documents were readily to hand, and there are limits to what may be done in only one month, but I have done the best I could."

"You could have asked Sharp for help," Reggie said. "He knows everything. He has been here since grandfather's day."

"Indeed, and Mr Sharp has been most willing to offer every assistance," Merton said. "However, I felt it best to view the original papers wherever possible, and not depend upon Mr Sharp's memory."

"His memory is perfectly sound," Reggie said. "He is not quite in his dotage yet."

"By no means. Indeed, I can well believe that Mr Sharp's acumen in matters of business is every bit as acute as it ever was. However, when one has been managing the affairs of one estate for three generations, there is a tendency for events to blend together somewhat, or for dates to be confused. It is my habit to refer to written records only, to avoid any such lapses in memory."

The marquess shuffled impatiently in his chair. "Reggie, I gave Merton a free hand to look into things, so there is no point quibbling about it now. Best to have a fresh perspective, you know. Take no notice of him, Merton. He is out of sorts because he thinks you will force me to sell off Marford House and all our hunters, but things are not so desperate as all that, surely? Are they?"

"No, no, but there are debts outstanding, and—"

"I am very sorry!" Monty burst out. "I will repay it all, I swear it! It was so foolish of me to buy those horses, and I shall find a way to—"

"Oh no, Lord Montague, none of the debts result from any action of yours," Merton said.

"Oh. Humphrey? Gil?"

Merton shook his head firmly. "I assure you, none of you are responsible."

"Then who is?" the marquess said sharply. "The fellow must be brought to to account. If there has been any misappropriation, I want it set right immediately and the scoundrel made to answer for it. Who is it?"

"The eighth Marquess of Carrbridge," Merton said.

There was a long, surprised silence.

"Father?" the marquess said. "You mean that Father left debts when he died, and they have not been settled?"

"That is correct."

"Well, that is easy enough. They must be settled at once... oh. There is no money to do so, that is the nub of the matter, I collect?"

"Exactly so, my lord."

The marchioness adjusted her shawl. "What must we do, Mr Merton? Advise us, if you please."

"My lady, my advice is very simple — to reduce unnecessary expenditure and to increase income. A few very modest economies will bring immediate benefits. For example, his lordship maintains five separate residences in London for the convenience of his brothers, while Marford House sits empty for months on end."

"What, must we have no independence now?" Reggie said. "Are we to be rubbing shoulders with the aunts all the time, and enduring their disapprobation whenever a fellow might happen to have a glass or two of brandy? It is not to be borne."

"Then there are three hunting lodges, where one would suffice," Merton went on relentlessly. "As for stabling—"

"I'll not have my hunters moved," Gus said, his voice so low he was almost growling. "Under no circumstances, do you hear me, Merton? Tell him, Carrbridge."

"Well—"

"My lady's plans for the new orangery could be postponed," Merton continued.

"Now that is more sensible," Reggie said.

"Indeed, it is not as if one needs to grow one's own oranges," Gus said. "It is the easiest thing in the world to have them sent from... well, wherever one obtains oranges. They can be had by the sack, I daresay, at very little expense. You can manage without an orangery, I am sure, Connie."

"I shall not give up my orangery unless you give up keeping all those teams at post houses," the marchioness said. "It is not as if one needs to keep one's own horses for the journey to London."

"What, drive around behind hired hacks?" Gus said, scandalised. "As the brother of a marquess, I have a position to maintain."

"You are the brother of an impoverished marquess," Merton said crisply, "and if you do not retrench— Ah, Lord Gilbert."

"Gil! At last!" Reggie said in relief, for so much talk of economy was beginning to wear at his nerves.

The youngest Marford brother tap-tapped his way across the library floor in a brisk rhythm. He was a handsome fellow — all his brothers were handsome, Reggie reflected gloomily. Carrbridge had more than once been likened to a Greek god, Humphrey was as big and golden as a bear, and the younger ones were fashionably dark and romantic, whereas Reggie had the face of a grocer. One of his Oxford friends had described him so, to his great mortification, and as he examined his uninteresting features in the glass later, he could not deny the truth of it.

"What is all this about, Merton?" Gil said. "I am missing a promising mill on your account, so I very much hope the matter is important."

"We are to give up two of the hunting lodges," Gus said. "Furthermore, we are not to stable our own teams at post houses."

"Ridiculous!" Gil said. "Impossible! How are we to manage?"

"There is worse," Reggie said. "We must give up our own lodgings and live in Marford House with the aunts."

"Insupportable!" Gil said. "I shall not listen to such nonsense."

He would have turned and left at once, but the marquess said, "Do not fly into the boughs, Gil. Something must be done, you know, for we have no money, it seems."

"How can that be?" Gil said. "We are one of the richest families in England."

"That is true, Carrbridge," Reggie said. "Grandfather was wont to boast that he had an income of twenty five thousand a year. Where has it gone to, that is what I should like to know. None of us is particularly extravagant. We do not gamble to excess or have—" He was about to mention mistresses before remembering the presence of two ladies. "We have no expensive interests," he finished lamely.

"It is a good point," the marquess said. "Where is all that money? We should be comfortably situated, heaven knows."

"Some of it is tied up in estates settled on various female relatives," Merton said. "The French holdings were lost a few years ago, so that accounts for a part of it, and the eighth marquess lost some profitable estates at the card tables. If you want my honest opinion, my lord, it is my belief that your income cannot sustain your present expenditure. I cannot be sure, because not all the relevant papers could be located, but I believe your current income does not exceed five thousand pounds a year."

They were all silent, contemplating this appalling state of poverty. Reggie had never thought much about money, for there had always seemed to be more than sufficient, but he knew that such a sum was inadequate to maintain them in their present style.

"What is to be done, Mr Merton?" the marchioness said. "You have mentioned some economies, but there must be more we can do."

"Indeed there is, my lady. There is a simple solution to the predicament. Lord Carrbridge's brothers might consider the options chosen by younger brothers for centuries, and take up respectable careers. Or, if they prefer, they might wish to marry women of independent means."

"Heiresses, I suppose," Reggie said in disgust. "So it is the church, the army or government service, or else get ourselves leg-shackled to some fish-faced cit's daughter. Lord, what a choice! I had rather become a pirate. Whatever are we to do?"

END OF SNEAK PREVIEW OF *Lord Reginald*

Find out more at http://marykingswood.co.uk

Printed in Dunstable, United Kingdom

76486219R00071